BLACK
DRAGON

*Also by W. E. Davis
in Large Print:*

Suspended Animation
Victim of Circumstance

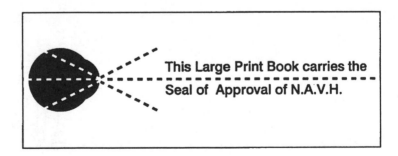

This Large Print Book carries the
Seal of Approval of N.A.V.H.

Black
Dragon

A Gil Beckman Mystery

W. E. Davis

Thorndike Press • Thorndike, Maine

Copyright © 1995 by W. E. Davis

Published in 1997 by arrangement with Crossway Books, a division of Good News Publishers.

Thorndike Large Print ® Christian Fiction Series.

The tree indicium is a trademark of Thorndike Press.

The text of this Large Print edition is unabridged.
Other aspects of the book may vary from the original edition.

Set in 16 pt. Plantin by Warren S. Doersam.

Printed in the United States on permanent paper.

Library of Congress Cataloging in Publication Data

Davis, Wally, 1951–
    Black dragon / W. E. Davis.
        p.   cm. — (A Gil Beckman mystery)
    ISBN 0-7862-1054-0 (lg. print : hc)
    I. Title.   II. Series: Davis, Wally, 1951–
Gil Beckman mystery.
[PS3554.A93785B53   1997]
813′.54—dc21   97-3983

To Royal and Suzi Kaji,
former residents of Minedoka, Idaho,
and to all former residents of
the Japanese internment camps.

One

This was not the same old moon I knew before.

Familiar images of inflated-looking space-men in white suits with gold-tinted face shields, bounding over the dusty surface leaving moon-shoe prints, picking up rocks, or hitting golf balls twelve miles, all blinked out when I was faced with the reality of being on the lunar surface myself.

My suit was much more streamlined than those of the Apollo astronauts, more resembling street clothes than their predecessors. As I moved out of the landing module my motion was unrestricted, and I was free to enjoy the light gravity. But I didn't have the time. My lunar rover awaited me, and I climbed into the small ground craft with my companion. Settling into the seats and snapping together the shoulder harness, we adjusted our special, lightweight visors and were ready to go. I tapped on the accelerator — a potentiometer for the electric motors — and we were in motion, rolling noiselessly across the irregular surface with the earth hanging in black space above us, blue, green, and brown, covered by swirls of pulled-apart cotton candy just as it appears in satellite photos.

But there the resemblance to the moon we all knew ended. No tranquil, distant place this moon; no sooner had we pulled away from the module than we were immediately assaulted by a hideous creature rising out of the sand in front of us. Its grotesque head whipped from side-to-side on a tremendous neck, covered with florescent skin like a snake, and its pointed snout opened into a gaping maw as it lunged toward us for the kill, three rows of irregular teeth dripping poisonous saliva that would most likely dissolve our clothing and us as we began our way down to its foul stomach.

But we were not caught unawares. I cranked the wheel to the left as my navigator took aim with a dash-mounted laser rifle, firing a quick burst into the exposed scaly neck of the beast.

Florescent green life fluid poured out of the gaping wound cut by the laser, and the creature screeched hideously, then slowly collapsed across our path in a cloud of low-gravity dust. I flicked the control wheel again and we drifted out of its way, victorious. But our joy was short-lived as we found ourselves on the loose edge of a small crater. Unable to avoid it, the rover's tires slipped downward off the edge toward the center of the depression — not the result of an errant meteor but the burrow of some other fantastic moon creature — where a pulsating mass of sand-like ooze bubbled hungrily for us, beckoning us to slide on down to our doom, machinery and all.

My partner would have none of this, however, and fired our right side boosters, small rockets whose force pushed the rover sideways and up over the rim, out of danger.

Before we could take a deep breath, a new problem arose on the horizon: three scout ships from the alien enemy's galaxy cruiser appeared in formation over the horizon, flying low on a recon mission directly toward us, for what profane purpose we couldn't begin to imagine. That they would soon see us and our landing module to our rear there was no doubt. We knew our only hope would be to blow them clean out of the . . . well, the sky.

But if they had a chance to radio our position to the mother ship before we smoked them, a second wave of fighter scouts would soon respond, and we would be doomed. Our only chance to prevent a further attack would be to take an aggressive posture and conduct a preemptive defensive strike. In other words, vaporize the buggers before they spotted us. And we would only have one shot.

We couldn't miss, not if we ever hoped to tread on terra firma again. To miss would tip them off and allow communication with their mother ship.

I flipped a red switch on the instrument panel, and the rover transformed instantly into the outer space equivalent of a mobile rocket launcher. I directed my navigator.

"Laser torpedoes activated."

"Check," she replied, her breathing hurried.

"Aim a little high. The surface of the moon is more curved than earth because it's smaller. They'll fly right into it. If they try to duck below our torpedoes they'll crash on the surface."

"Check."

"On my mark. . . . Fire!"

Four greenish fireballs streamed from tubes above our heads, staying close to the moon's surface; so close they stirred up dust. Their trail was long, extending all the way back to us no matter how far the torpedoes flew. Indeed, their power source was on board the rover and they had to remain "tethered," as it were. Such was the nature of lasers.

That laser beams always travel in a straight line was a problem only recently conquered. They could be arced by restricting the flow at one point on their edges which would cause the beam to bend in that direction, something like an archery bow when it is strung. The more the restriction, the bigger the arc.

If the bow string breaks, the tension whips both ends of the bow violently. With the laser, the straightening process must also be gradual, or the rover — one end of the bow — would be flung upward. So laser-bending is discouraged by the Space Administration.

But the S. A. wasn't on the moon about to get turned into a tiny puff of smoke and microscopic fragments. We needed that arc in the beams to avoid straightline discovery: an arcing laser is invisible to detectors. Only at the last possible moment could we ease off the arc by releasing the restrictors on the lower aspects of the beams, allowing them to home in on the quarry. I counted down.

"One . . . two . . . now!"

My companion turned the dial to the left slowly, deliberately, fighting her fear and the urge to get it over with, to flip the dial and waste the fighter scouts. But she did it right, then we watched as the torpedoes were spotted by the fighters, who peeled off in different directions. But too late, as the laser-guided torpedoes sensed their targets and disconnected themselves from the guidance beams and found their marks, and three nearly simultaneous fireballs exploded silently in the zero atmosphere above the lunar surface.

There was no time for rejoicing. We were surprised by a fourth fireball. The final torpedo had struck a fighter we had not seen, one that had been tailing the others at a distance. It was destroyed, but had the alien pilot been able to signal our location to its mother ship?

It had. The mother ship suddenly appeared on the horizon and a green tractor beam locked onto our small rolling craft. We could not resist and were sucked into the gigantic ship, as large as a city block and covered with pipes and plates and hatches and doors and lights and other gizmos. A door opened and we were soon inside the beast. Dark, smelling lightly of sulfur and steam, it filled us with a sense of foreboding. Then, without any warning, lights came on, and a world of science and fiction erupted around us. Alien creatures, robots, fantastic machinery, bizarre noises, strange music, *gloop* sounds.

But no, I can tell you no more. You'll have to experience it for yourself.

Our ride was soon ended. Trish and I were

breathless and excited as our rover docked in the blue lights of the landing zone and we were helped out of it by a female teenager in a black spandex body suit with a red diagonal stripe across her chest. She said she hoped we liked our adventure on Moonraiders and enjoyed the rest of our day at the park.

I admired her uniform. When Trish caught me at it she gave me an elbow in the side.

"I'll tell Sally," she threatened.

"Those outfits were your idea," I rejoined.

"Yeah, but they're just for the promotion. The regular, permanent costumes will be more modest so people besides models can work here. They'll be the same idea, only a little baggier."

"Rats," I said. "I mean, good."

Michelle Yokoyama, senior vice president of the themed amusement park, met us at the end of the unloading ramp. Her hair was ever so slightly disheveled, and she smiled broadly.

"Wow!" she said with an exhale. "That was great!"

I agreed. Trish just concentrated on breathing.

"What did you guys get into?" Michelle asked.

I told her, and she related her experience, which had been different.

"That virtual reality thing was awesome!" Trish gasped, her eyes still wide.

"Semi-virtual reality," I corrected. "It's not like a video game, where our input dictates everything, but it has the feel that we are in control."

"And it's definitely different every time you ride," Trish said. "I went on it five times this morning. I'd say it's ready for the grand opening."

"How does it work, anyway?" Michelle asked.

"Magic," I said.

"Stop it, Gil," Trish scolded. "It's the visor. They project the different scenarios directly onto it, with hundreds of choices, and it's done randomly. It can be different every time you ride."

"You've ruined it for me," I said. "I thought it was magic."

"That's a brilliant marketing idea," Michelle said. "People will want to ride it over and over."

"Thank you," I said.

"That wasn't your idea," Trish reminded me.

"Oh? You sure?"

"That was all part of the original plan," Trish explained to Michelle. "Of course, the folks in Design and Planning carried it out."

"And Jerry Opperman will take credit for it," I prophesied.

"Oh, here comes Jerry now," Michelle said, ignoring me and looking past us up the exit ramp. "Let's hear what he thinks."

"Who cares what he thinks?" I whispered to Trish, who fisted me on the arm and gave me a look that clearly said *shut up*.

Opperman, the president of the theme park, and Security Chief Harry Clark staggered down the ramp together, their faces marked by insipid grins under furrowed brows — the classic expression of relieved terror.

"I can *see* what he thinks," I said.

They stopped when they got to us and other department heads and supervisors who had also just emptied out of the ride gathered themselves in an impromptu circle around us.

Harry Clark shook my hand.

"Great job, Gil. Just great."

"Thanks, Harry, but all I did was supervise. The hero is the guy who thought it up and the people who made it happen."

"Yes, yes," echoed Opperman hastily. "We want to congratulate the designers. This ride is fantastic. A home run! This is the greatest thing ever to happen to amusement parks. Nothing like this has been done before. It'll revolutionize the industry. From the day I suggested implementing the plan. . . ."

He droned on from there, and I eyed Trish and Michelle with skepticism. Michelle winked, and Trish shook her head once. I stared at Jerry incredulously, but he avoided my gaze, per usual.

Opperman had opposed the plan from the beginning, although only tacitly, since the owners' group was heartily in favor of the upgrades, new rides, expansion, and the new direction the park would be taking. He went along, at first acting as a stumbling block because none of the ideas were his, then slowly began to assume a more active and positive role in an attempt to wrest credit away from those more deserving.

How do I know all this? Well, what I couldn't surmise, or figure out from circumstances, I learned from . . . let's just say an informed source. A good cop always has his informants.

I had overseen the development of the plan — not as supervisor, really, but more like an ombudsman with authority, since I had no particular expertise in the field. Kind of a policeman of sorts, to make sure what they did followed the guidelines. It had been going on for a year now. Moonraiders was finished, two other indoor rides were being refurbished and renovated, and one other ride — a roller coaster — was completed and in the final testing stage. But the most important part of the Plan, as we called it, was the introduction of a new character, a mascot. He would be the unifying force that tied the whole place into a single cohesive unit.

The little dinosaur, a pear-shaped, upright-walking, anthropomorphic apatasaur, who had a time machine (that's how he got here; he found it unattended in a swamp), and could turn up anywhere in the park in the clothing of that area. Sometimes it was only a hat, but it did the trick. The American West, the Roaring 20s, medieval Europe, outer space. Whatever or wherever, he was there. And he showed up on the shelves of the stores and souvenir shops as well, in games, on shirts, mugs, stuffed toys, collectibles. You name it, he was on it. And he predated that nauseating purple goody-two-shoes on TV — by several years, too.

Everett (he was named after his creator) had also recently debuted in the newspapers as a panel strip in the funnies, to positive, albeit cautious, reviews. Afraid that he was just a ploy to cash in on the merchandising, most critics took a wait-and-see attitude. Joey Duncan, the kid hired to draw the strips, turned out to have some good ideas for Everett and had a young person's viewpoint that gave a certain edge to the dinosaur. He had his problems coping with the world (Everett, that is, although Joey had his share as well), but with the time machine he could travel around looking for solutions.

Granted, not very Christian or realistic, but at least he didn't just sit around all day eating lasagna or sleeping on top of his house like some of his contemporaries.

Though not given signature credit in the strips — not yet at least, since Joey was on probation in the position and still just an employee of the park — Joey soon came to realize the experience he gained here would get him a foot in some door later, perhaps with his own strip or animated cartoon. Once that lightbulb blinked on over his head, he threw himself into his task with fervor, and his delinquency problems subsided.

That God and I were keeping an eye on him probably contributed to it also.

I said good-bye to Trish, who returned to Design and Planning with her compatriots. As I walked back with Michelle to her office inside the Bijou Theater complex in the Flapper Zone — she had finally moved into the office there vacated by the former senior V. P. and given me use of her old office trailer temporarily — I listened to her discuss her vision for the future of the park. It was obvious to me then that my stint in this position would soon be drawing to a close. Trish, creative in her own right, could assimilate into Design and Planning. But an ex-cop who still carried his park security badge could not do so, and it was only a matter of time before I'd be returned to my former duties in the brown and khaki uniform of the security guard.

I had no background or experience that qualified me for a management position here. Harry Clark was firmly entrenched as security chief, a job I didn't think I'd really like anyway. There was too much schmoozing and posterior kissing to suit me. And I didn't have the temperament to be a yes man. God gave me a personality — some folks at church referred to it as a spiritual gift — that liked to call things what they were, to see issues in black and white, to discern quickly the true nature of people.

That, coupled with a carnal tendency to shoot off my mouth, created a dangerous quagmire under me at all times that threatened to swallow me at the slightest provocation. I sometimes couldn't hold my peace, especially if my opinion had been sought. I didn't pull punches, or agree verbally when

I disagreed internally. I called things what they were. To do otherwise was to lie, and that's a sin. If you don't want to know the truth, then don't ask me, I would always say.

Needless to say, as time went by, I ticked off a few fellow travelers along the road of life.

I wasn't disappointed about my future. I knew it was coming and had even prepared myself mentally. I was learning to be content in whatever state I found myself, knowing that God would put me where He wanted me.

But I wasn't looking forward to it. Don't think that for a minute. I enjoyed the position I was in, reporting directly to the senior vice president, coordinating the efforts of several groups of people, making decisions, getting to explore the rides and the whole park — amusement area and backstage — at will. And getting paid fair money to do so.

The handwriting was on the wall, however. *Mene mene chili beanie* — no, wait, that wasn't right. It was *tekel upharsin,* "Thou art weighed in the balance and found wanting." In my case, I was found wanting something to do. And going back to security seemed to be it.

We arrived, and Michelle led me into her

lair — I mean, office. I flopped into a leather chair, and she got a soda for each of us out of the little refrigerator in the corner.

"It's not enough that we're under a push to be ready for the grand opening of the new rides," she lamented between sips. "I just found out from Jerry this morning we've got a V.I.P. coming on Saturday."

"So?" I said, inspecting the moisture on the outside of the can. "We have V.I.P.s all the time. Who is it this time? Some has-been movie star? The governor's sister? Lady Di's manicurist? Anybody from *Happy Days*?"

"Nobody you'd know offhand, perhaps," Michelle explained. "But you'll know the name. Kumi Hiromoto."

"As in Hiro Industries? Automobiles, shipping, tall pointy buildings in every major commercial center in this country?"

"He owns a good chunk of every major city in this country."

"What in the world is he doing here? Don't tell me, he's in love with our frozen bananas, right?"

"Could be. We're negotiating to build a new park like this one outside Nagasaki. He's the major funder. His business, that is."

"Hiro Industries is going to bankroll a duplicate park like this in Japan?" I shook my head. "I hope they don't want one exactly

21

like this. Given the opportunity to start over, they could at least have a few things redesigned to make sense."

"That's the plan. The Japanese are very concerned about everything being just so, and there not being any bugs."

"They want to save face, is that it?"

"Well, yes, I suppose. Not that the rest of us don't, it's just that the Japanese are particularly concerned about it."

At first, when she said this, I chuckled inside; Michelle being Japanese, speaking as if she weren't. Then I thought about it and realized she wasn't Japanese; she was an American who just happened to be of Japanese ancestry.

"When things go wrong here," I said, "the person who is responsible can just blame someone else. That's how we save face."

Michelle nodded. "Unhappily true."

"Is Opperman involved in this deal?"

"Yes, but the owners are doing their best to keep him in check. They don't think the Japanese would understand his eccentricities."

"We don't, why should they?"

Michelle smiled. "You know, Gil, you're considered eccentric by most people . . . those who don't know you well, at least."

"I'm not eccentric, I'm just intense."

"I'm sure Jerry thinks he's absolutely normal, too."

"Yeah, well . . . whatever." I waved her off. "So tell me more about Hiromoto. I'm surprised he's coming himself. Doesn't he have people to send?"

"Oh, they've already been here. He's a real hands-on kind of guy. He's seventy, and still makes every major decision himself. It's the —"

"Don't tell me, it's the Japanese way."

She only smiled. "And get this," she continued. "He's an absolute fan of Everett. He thinks the little dinosaur is the funniest thing he's ever seen. He wants to meet him personally."

I hooted. "He understands it's just a guy in a suit, doesn't he? A cartoon in 3-D?"

"I'm sure he does. But he wants to believe, Gil. Just like the kid in all of us."

Not in me, I thought. "Well, for that kind of money," I said, "I'd give him a grilled sandwich made with green cheese from the moon if he wanted to believe it." I caught myself, stunned by my own idea, and gave Michelle a funny look. "There you go. The new eatery outside Moonraiders. Green-cheese-from-the-moon grilled sandwiches, with thin-sliced ham; patty melts; craters of fries; Tang in tubes; moon rock candy at the souvenir cart. . . ."

"You're a genius, Gil."

I didn't respond. What could I say?

"Security's going to be the big concern," Michelle said, getting back to the subject.

"Why don't they just bring him in when we're closed?"

She shook her head. "He wants to spend the day, experience the ambiance of the park on a normal day."

"As soon as he shows up with his entourage and Jerry and Harry start running around like whirling dervishes, it'll cease to be a normal day. Besides the park doesn't have ambiance. Dark, pricey restaurants have ambiance."

Michelle grinned. "Atmosphere, then."

"Atmosphere it has," I consented.

"I'm sure Harry will be speaking to you about it."

"Excuse me? He wants me to guard this guy? On my day off?"

"Not exactly. He's got a plan formulated. He just wants you to go over it, see if there's something obvious he missed. I think he's also going to ask you to take it to Mr. Hiromoto's grandson —"

"Grandson?"

"Yes. Eric Hiromoto."

"What is he, ten or something?"

24

"No. Eric Hiromoto's in his late twenties. He's heir to the empire since his father was killed in a plane crash. Remember that last year?"

"The one that slammed into Mt. Fuji?"

"Yes. Eric was raised here, went to Stanford, has offices in San Francisco and Los Angeles."

"You've done your homework." I smiled knowingly. "Might he be single?"

She shot me a perturbed stare. "He's ten years younger than me, and I'm not interested. Besides, I've had my fill of Japanese businessmen."

"Sorry. I forgot about that for a minute."

"That's okay. I know you were only kidding around. But, just for the record, he doesn't know me from Eve, and it wouldn't be any of your business if he did."

"I better go see Harry," I said, "before I get any deeper."

I left Michelle with a wave, deciding a reflective and rejuvenating walk through the park before seeing Harry would be a healthy thing. I figured I might even pop over to the Dragon and see if they were feeding it yet.

Two

Feeding the Dragon. That's the term the ride operators used for loading passengers onto the new roller coaster. So far, all they'd been able to say was "*When* are we going to feed the dragon?" It was still being tested, but they hoped to open it Saturday, and now I knew the significance of choosing that day.

The Dragon. So named because of its serpentine track but more so because of the way it breathed fire and devoured its prey. This was the latest volley in the roller coaster wars and, as such, was greatly anticipated by the press and those members of the public who couldn't find enough ways to get their thrills.

It was one aspect of the makeover of the park that Everett Curran's plan had not described in detail, just in principle. Ostensibly the brainchild of Jerry Opperman, I thought it more likely the product of the guy in Design and Planning who drew the blueprints. Opperman wasn't this big of a thinker. He was a talker, which is why he had hung on this long as president. He could flimflam the owners. A couple of them, sweet little old ladies who couldn't see through his charade, he had in his pocket.

The folks in D. and P., to their credit, had done a fairly remarkable job on the make-over, considering most of the ideas weren't theirs. The park was beginning to have a more unified feeling; instead of separate themed zones butted up next to each other, they were tied in by one basic theme — time travel. Rather than being a patchwork quilt of disassociated lands created by the whim of a dyslexic god, it was now a single jump-ing-off place where many different places and times could be visited without having to give up your parking space.

No more did one zone start where the adjoining one stopped. The park guests were now time travelers themselves, able to trans-port along with Everett from one era to an-other with a flash of strobe lights as they walk between zones, giving the sensation of being transported in the twinkling of an eye. One step, you're in prehistoric times. Step *flash* step, you are standing on the edge of the American West.

They even arranged the hidden speakers for the piped-in mood music in such a way that, as your visual senses were affected by the strobe of the time machine, the back-ground music abruptly changed as well. And, since time travel would make it possible, each area had its own Everett in the appropriate costume. The kids were mystified and delighted.

In a kind of no-man's-land between medieval Europe and Camp Wilderness, the Dragon made its lair. This was a roller coaster with a twist — a literal twist. At one point it shoots up rather steeply, flung by aircraft carrier catapults, but instead of cresting and coming back down, the track twists and turns on its axis so the cars essentially do a roll-over, ending momentarily upside down before a reverse downward curve that sends the riders back the other way, then around a sweeping banked curve that slopes downward to pick up speed, darts briefly upward, then levels off so suddenly as the track drops imperceptibly that for a few moments you think you are flying.

Then *wham!* you reconnect and are thrust into a sideways turn and through a series of "S" curves, each banked toward the inside and opposite of each other, then cruise into the station and come to an abrupt halt, out of breath and ready to disembark before your legs have caught up with you.

So they tell me. Thus far no one had actually ridden on it.

It would not be for the faint of heart or

the weak of stomach. In fact, the Dragon carried a height and physical condition disclaimer. *Don't ride the Dragon unless you have made peace with your God.* Something like that.

There it was, looming ahead of and over me, a twisting mass of fire-belching black steel. Once a minute a screeching train of empty metal and fiberglass cars lurched and slammed through the loops and up and down the inclines as the ride was tested and retested in preparation for its unveiling. Testosterone-injected teenage boys stood on the pathway nearest the monster, drooling.

I stopped by a newly landscaped area at the base of one of the steel support posts to watch. The park's horticulturist — landscape designer/gardener/green thumb/whatever you want to call him — was putting the finishing touches on a flower bed that decorated the otherwise useless area beneath the ride, hiding the concrete footings.

"So, what do you think, Mr. Ozawa?" I asked him.

The small, ageless, Asian-American man squinted up at me from under a baseball cap, shrugged, then went back to work, patting the dirt around the base of a plant and pinching off a few leaves.

"Noisy," he said, no expression on his face.

"True. But what isn't around here?"

"These," he said motioning lightly at his garden.

"They're beautiful."

He moved to another plant. "Yes," he sighed. I couldn't read his intent. He sounded almost sad, sorry that his precious plants had to be here, languishing virtually unnoticed at the base of some roller coaster, unappreciated by the masses whose priority was finding new ways to part with their lunch. They should have been adorning the garden area of an art museum.

To me they were just plants, something that covered dirt and required a lot of work.

I moved off, simultaneously amused and touched by the landscaper. Every person has to have something that is important to them, more important than just about anything else. For this gentleman, that something was his plants. They may have belonged to the park, but they were his.

I wondered what his home looked like. I imagined he had a house or yard full of *bonsai*, but caught myself, realizing I was stereotyping him. For all I knew he was a model railroader at home, or an amateur chef. Maybe he got enough of plants and dirt at work and when he was lounging around the house he did crosswords or collected John

Wayne movies. When I went home I didn't solve mysteries. If he had any plants at all, they were probably plastic.

I glanced back as I wandered away, but he was gone, off to cultivate the earth elsewhere. I had to admire his work. The planter areas under the Dragon were themed: Japanese gardens, with rock streams and exotic blooms; southwestern United States, with cactus and succulents and those purple things — lupins I think they're called. There were no straight lines in the borders, but broad, sweeping curves and mounds that led the eye. The colors were intense and purposeful, transitioning gradually through the spectrum in proper rainbow order as the eye circumnavigated the landscape. They were in sharp contrast to the flat black of the steel Dragon.

Each planter, and there were many under the ride, was unique, both in shape and content, and they were isolated from each other by small ponds filled with *koi* or puddles of thick, green grass or rock formations, or combinations of all three.

The park used to cover these areas with painted asphalt and ice cream carts. Things were looking up.

The thunderous clattering of the Dragon roaring overhead drew my attention skyward. Watching the carts fly past, I mounted the steps to the loading platform and control center and stood at the fringe of a group of ride maintenance people. Dave Whelan, head of the Rides Division, stood at the simple controls and sent the string of empty cars off as soon as they had come to rest. He looked like a kid with a new electric train, trying his darndest to break it.

Of course, that's the way to test a new ride before you put people on it. Do everything you can to make it fail. The designers and engineers can test it in principle on computers and with models, but the dynamics are just not the same as the real thing.

And so the empty cars continued to fly around overhead, sounding eerie without the screams of humans and empty without the mass of bodies to muffle the metallic sounds.

Dave Whelan saw me and nodded a greeting.

"You're just in time," he said.

"Yeah? What for?"

"For the inaugural run." He brought the carts to rest at the loading platform. I waited patiently, knowing he was going to illuminate. A wry grin bent the corners of his mouth up.

"Want to go for a ride?"

"Is it ready for humans?" I asked, not that I was interested.

He nodded. "Been testing it nonstop for two days. Design and Planning's coming by to take her for a spin. I'm sure they'll let you on too."

"They'll have to pay me." I stood my ground. "Besides, this is their thing. I didn't have anything to do with the Dragon. Let them have the first ride all to themselves." *First, last, and every one in between,* I mentally added.

"Aw, come on, Gil," said a female voice behind me. "Don't be a chicken."

"I'm not being a chicken, Trish," I said without looking back. "I . . . uh, just ate." I had — only three hours before.

I wasn't afraid of the speed, or the sudden turns. I wasn't afraid of the height, not really. In fact, I wasn't even afraid of falling. It was the sudden-stop landings that always hurt people. Cement poisoning. Sudden deceleration syndrome.

One night, back when I was still in uniform, I had tried to walk up the metal stairway adjacent to the first incline of another roller coaster here. I was fine when I started, but the higher I went the harder it got to take that next step. My legs got heavier, gravity stronger, and I just knew I was going to slip between the treads to my doom. I finally had to back down, not even a third of the way up. Okay, maybe I was a little afraid of heights.

"It'll only take a few seconds," Trish pleaded.

"That's about how long it takes me to get car sick."

"Aw, you're just a lightweight, Gil. Big, tough, hard-boiled detective . . . my eye."

That did it, she'd pushed me to the limit. There was only one thing I could do.

"Okay," I admitted. "So I'm a lightweight. Have a good time."

"I can't even goad you into riding?" Trish asked.

"Nope."

"Come on, big guy," Joey Duncan mocked, joining the peer pressure group. "You're always acting so tough."

"Only compared to you, kid."

Joey snorted and walked over to the control panel so Whelan could show him how it worked. Before taking over the cartooning chores Joey had been a ride operator.

"Now I'm really not going, not if he's driving," I said.

"Don't worry, man, I'm just going to watch," Joey explained.

Trish took my arm and held it firmly.

"Well, if we can't talk you into it, I guess we'll just have to force you. Come on, guys."

A dire predicament I was in now. Where she held my arm, I'd embarrass both of us if I tried to move it. I gave in as the rest of the Design and Planning folk pressed around, laughing and joking, and swept me into the lead car with Trish. She went in first, hauling me behind her. She only let go when the padded shoulder harness was lowered over us and locked in place, and I was committed. I glared at her playfully — but meaning it — and wished out loud she was my daughter.

"Why?" she asked.

"So I could ground you for a month and take away your telephone privileges."

She laughed freely, the way people do when they know they've got the upper hand. I grumbled.

There were five carts, four to a cart, allowing twenty people to ride at once. The back seat of our cart was empty, as were several other seats in the string. There were twelve or thirteen of us on the ride.

A buzzer sounded, something below us clanked, and we jerked into motion as a heavy chain grabbed the pin on the bottom of the cart and dragged us out of the loading area and up the steep first incline.

This part of the ride was great. A slow ascent to the second highest point in the park — the Cloud Tickler, a revolving observation tower being the highest — during which we had a brief but fantastic view of virtually the whole park. I ventured a peek over the side, admiring the symmetry and beauty of the landscaper's handiwork, and picking out the garden I most preferred losing my breakfast in later, then gave Trish one more hard look as we crested the top.

"If I die, I'll kill you," I threatened.

She just laughed and raised her arms, transforming her carefree giggle into a scream as we were released and began our speedy descent into the afterlife.

The first half of the ride wasn't too bad, actually. Vertical loops aren't as bad for the rider as they appear to the spectator. Riders just have the sensation they are going up continuously while the scenery changes perspective, then suddenly they straighten out again.

The ride was a mite better than a root canal. Trish screamed in delight the whole way, as did some of the folks behind me — those who hadn't fallen out. Before I knew it we were on our way up the final incline. As we crested the apex I heard a strange pop, a distinctly different sound than any I'd heard before. It was barely audible above Trish's screeching, and she didn't seem to notice.

But I couldn't discount it. It was too close, and sounded as if it had come from directly beneath me. This all happened in a split second, of course, and before I had a chance to do anything — not that there was anything I could have done — there was a grating noise, and the groan of stretching steel, as our cart suddenly shifted and dropped down onto the track at an odd angle. Trish's scream changed to one of surprise and terror, which was repeated behind us by male and female voices. My mind of its own will formed a final prayer, but it wasn't of much substance, mostly a cry of *Here I come, Lord!* as the carts to the rear slammed into us when friction slowed our cart down.

Something underneath caught on the track or the framework, and our nonparallel angle to the track increased. We slowed to the shriek of metal-to-metal contact, the front portion of our cart hanging precariously out over nothing as the whole train ground to a halt at a place in the track that was more or less level, held in place by the mass of deformed metal underneath.

It was also the highest place in the track, and the view was at the same time breathtaking and frightening.

Even as people shouted and screamed, I took inventory. Remarkably, we were all still alive. No one had fallen out, thanks to the harness system, but there were undoubtedly some bumps and bruises. I thanked the Lord the accident had occurred here, on a relatively flat spot in the track. Anywhere else and we'd have been subject to gravity and either fallen out or left the track completely.

I tried to calm Trish down. She was panicking completely as she ventured a cautious glance over the side of the cart and had an unobstructed view of the ground several stories below. There was nothing between her and eternity except a frail aluminum and fiberglass bucket held in place by damaged metal, friction, and a prayer.

Behind me, several avowed atheists quickly and audibly appealed to the God they didn't believe existed. I wished I had a tape recorder, knowing they would probably deny it later.

I shouted for everyone to calm down and remain still.

"Don't move! Any movement could break us free! Help is on the way!"

I hoped. There were only two ways to get us down: helicopter or cherry picker — those bucket things the electric companies and fire departments use. But either one would take some time. I didn't know how long we could last — how long the cart would remain in this delicate position.

Trish gripped the solid shoulder harness until her knuckles lost all color. She cried freely.

"I should have gone to England!" she wailed.

"What?"

"With my parents."

"Oh. Well, Trish, there's nothing we can do about it now. We're going to be okay, they'll get us down. Just try to be still, please."

"I don't want to die, Gil."

"Well, neither do I, hon," I admitted. I didn't think quoting Paul, *to live is Christ, to die is gain,* would be a good idea at the moment. "God will protect us. Just trust in Him, okay?"

"I'm sorry, Gil. It's my fault."

"Your fault? You didn't do anything."

"I made you get on the ride," she whimpered.

That's true, I thought. But what I said was, "Nah, I could have stayed off if I really wanted to. I was just playing around." No sense adding to her guilt right now. And that was the truth, I could have stayed off the ride. But someone would've gotten hurt if I'd tried.

"Sally's going to hate me!" She sobbed, crying with renewed fervor.

"Good grief, Trish, why do you say that?" I stole a glance over the side and felt a weakness crawling up my legs as the blood rushed to my head.

"If anything happens to you —"

"Nothing's going to happen to me — or you either, for that matter. Now get a grip! The best thing you can do right now is pray . . . and hold on."

I chanced a look down and off to my right, seeing the alarmed crowd gathering below. The cart rocked slightly in the wind, held in place by I didn't know what, and I feared it could break loose any second, dropping us and possibly everyone else as well to our deaths. My heart pounded and adrenaline pumped, giving me the shakes, and the weakness in my legs had reached all the way up, going now into my hips.

"Dear God," I breathed.

I turned my head slowly to look over my shoulder. "Is everyone okay?"

There were a few nods, one or two affirmative answers, but mostly staccato breathing and sobbing. A woman prayed in Spanish. A few nursed their heads, one man held a bloody handkerchief to his forehead and stared straight ahead with glazed eyes. Another man — whom I believed to have been the primary designer of the Dragon — kept shaking his head and muttering that he didn't understand. The woman next to him glared at him accusingly.

I took Trish's hand, first having to pry it off the bar. It was icy cold as she gripped me hard enough to break bones, and I remembered our first meeting at the ice skating rink where she'd gone to remember happier times. I thought that, even as wealthy as her parents were, there was no escaping the great equalizer — death — whether it be your own or a loved one's.

I thought, too, of Sally as I looked out over the city from my lofty and rather tenuous perch, and realized suddenly I had indeed fallen in love with her. Bad choice of words, I told myself, but that's what I thought. I had actually grown into love with her. "Fallen" implies a sudden, uncontrolled thing, which it wasn't. I even fought it off as I tried to remain true to Rachel, my wife, my partner, whom I'd known since my teen years and married at twenty, only to lose her a few years back to a mysterious illness. Even I, the great Gil Beckman, world's best sleuth, couldn't solve that one.

41

It wasn't until I realized that it wasn't betraying Rachel for me to learn to love again; God had a purpose in taking her and leaving me here — even if I didn't know what that purpose was — and he had a purpose in bringing Sally and me together.

A lot goes through your mind very quickly when death is imminent, some of it involuntarily, some of it on purpose to overcome the fear. I'd be lying if I said I wasn't afraid. It was all I could do not to panic, but for Trish's sake I needed to remain at least outwardly calm. I wanted to cry and beg God to snatch us miraculously out of the carts and set us on solid ground, but I knew He wouldn't. Not mystically, anyway. So I prayed He would hold the carts in place until a rescue could be mounted.

What I didn't expect was a nearby voice to call my name.

"Mr. Beckman!" It took a second to register and I didn't respond. Again, "Mr. Beckman!" Yes, there was no doubt. It was Joey Duncan's voice, and it was coming from right below us.

Three

I leaned back and peeked over the rear of the cart.

Joey, with a stout rope coiled over one shoulder bandolier-style, was climbing the steel framework.

Trish heard him too, but was afraid to look down.

"Who's that?" she asked. "What's going on?"

"Joey's climbing up," I said. "I don't know for sure what he's up to, but it can't be he's going to try to haul us down himself. I think he might be planning to cinch the cart down so it can't slip anymore."

"He's crazy!" Trish whimpered.

In a minute Joey was directly beneath us.

"What're you doing?" I asked him.

"You guys all okay?"

"So far. A few minor injuries, some new gray hairs, lots of frayed nerves. Are they bringing some equipment in?"

"Yeah, the fire department has a ladder truck that'll almost reach."

"Almost."

"Yeah. You're not too high, technically, but they can't get the truck close enough for the ladder to reach even at full extension because of the angle caused by the path being so far away. We need you down there." He pointed with one hand to a lower portion of the track, while hanging on with the other. He was fearless. Even when I was his age I wouldn't have been that cool.

"What's your plan?" I asked, hoping and praying he hadn't come up here without one.

"I've got to get you two out of that car, uncouple it, and let it fall so we can winch the rest of the carts down slowly to where the ladder can reach them."

"I hope you don't mind me saying so, Joey, but neither of us are up to climbing out."

"Yeah, I thought that might be the case. That's why I brought the rope. First, I have to cable off the rear cart. Hold on for a minute, would you?"

I thought of several witty and sarcastic things to say in response, like "Do we have to?" or "Thanks for telling us, we were about to jump out," but somehow I just didn't have the necessary energy. In a second Joey had ducked out of sight beneath us. I could hear him as he clambered around on this overgrown erector set and in a minute heard him shout down to someone below to tie the rope

44

to the cable hook and he'd haul it back up. He shouted for some slack, and I heard the clanking of the cable and Joey's grunts as he hauled it back in. Then he connected one end of the cable to the rear cart.

"Okay," he shouted down, "take it in just a little to make it tight . . . slowly! Okay, stop!" There was the slightest of jerks as the cable became taut and Trish yelped, but I held her arm and tried to soothe her.

"It's okay, we're tied down now. We can't go anywhere." I hoped that was completely true, but I knew what was yet to come, and I wasn't looking forward to it.

I had rapelled several years back when I was on the police department S.W.A.T. team, down the sides of water tanks and short buildings and out of helicopters, but never really liked it. And this was a bit different anyway, since I wasn't wearing a harness. But we had to get out of this damaged cart before anything else could happen.

Then the cart string could be eased down the track. Actually, gravity would do the work once our broken cart was separated. The cable was to hold them back, keep them from freewheeling. They could then be let slowly and safely down to where the firemen would be waiting and could pluck us off one by one.

But that could only happen when our damaged car was released and out of the way, and that wasn't going to occur until Trish and I were safely out of it.

We rocked gently in the breeze, unable to enjoy the view as we were ever mindful how tenuous our grasp on life was at that moment.

"Gil?" Trish asked, her voice cracking.

"Yeah?"

"Can I tell you something?"

"Sure."

"I — I hate to admit this, but if we don't —"

"Shhh. We'll be fine. Don't even think about it."

"I'm scared, Gil. I don't know if . . . what I wanted to say is, I think you're . . . I had a —"

We jerked a little and she sucked back the rest of her comment with her breath. I patted her leg in a fatherly fashion to reassure her. It was quivering.

"I had a crush on you," she blurted out.

I immediately pulled my hand away. "Well, thanks, Trish. I'll admit, there were times I wished I was nineteen."

"Thank you for saying so and I —" Her answer was overcome by a scream as our cart shifted, tipping another six inches to the side then jerking to a stop, forcing me to hold my breath sharply and retain it until I was sure we were done moving. *That's another year off my life now*, I thought. When I regained my composure I searched frantically for Joey. How long would this take? At that moment a rope flung itself over the edge of the cart, startling us.

"Put it around her waist!" Joey yelled. "Then she can climb back into the next car!"

Joey was behind us, on top of the track. He had cabled the string of cars off and was ready to let ours loose, once we were out of it. The front seat in the second car was empty as the man in it had moved to the rear and was holding on to the woman already there.

"How do we get out of the shoulder harness?" I asked.

"Just push up. I already hit the emergency release button on the back of the cart," Joey explained, "then all you have to do is crawl back here. It'll be over in five minutes." Indeed, the fire truck had arrived and was being positioned. Its ladder would be up and ready by the time we were down the track.

"Easier said than done, kid," I said, then leaned over to Trish. "Sweetheart, you're going to have to help me now. You've got to tie this rope around you and crawl back to the next car."

47

She looked up at me with the widest eyes I've ever seen on a non-marsupial.

"It's just a few feet," I added. "Like crawling over the couch at home. You can make it."

Her chin began to quiver, and she didn't move.

"Come on, Trish," Joey yelled.

"Trish, you must," I urged. "We've got to get out of this cart. There's no other way. God will take care of you." I pushed up the shoulder harness as Joey instructed and Trish held her breath. Then I looped the rope, slipped it over her head and put her arms through it, just like dressing a little kid, and pulled it taut, making sure it wouldn't loosen. All the while she just looked at me like I was preparing to throw her to the lions. Maybe I was, but I had no choice. I didn't think the cart could hold much longer.

Truth be known, I was probably as scared as she was, but if I did what I felt like doing — wailing at the top of my lungs and turning into Jell-O — we were doomed. So I gulped the lump back down my throat and said another prayer, and cinched the rope around her waist.

Trish forced herself to look over her shoulder. Her climb would not only be toward the back, but up, for our cart was off the track

48

at an angle and yielding to gravity.

"I'll keep the rope tight so you can't slide back," Joey said. "Come on, Trish, hurry!"

"I can't!" she cried.

"Yes you can, Trish!" someone in a cart at the rear shouted. "Please, we all want to get down!"

"Yes!" urged a woman. "God will protect you."

"You're beautiful," I told her. "You're going to be fine, and one day that special someone will come into your life, and you'll fall in love and get married and have kids, and this will be just an exciting story to tell your little twins, Joey and Gilbert." She cracked an involuntary, nervous smile. "But first," I continued, "you have to get out of this cart. Trust God — and me and Joey — and climb."

"O-okay," she said weakly. "Hold me!"

"I've got you."

Biting her lip, Trish tried again. I steadied her, then with my hand on her back turned and grabbed the back of the cart.

"Pull up," Joey said, taking out the slack in the rope as she did so. I turned in my seat, wedging my feet firmly in the bottom of the cart, and kept my hand on her, for psychological support as much as anything. If she decided to let go there was no way I could stop her.

"Don't look down," Joey said. "Keep your eyes on me."

"That's it," I urged as she inched her way up. Joey reeled her in like a trout, keeping the rope taut. Soon she was on the back of the cart, a foot or two from her destination.

"Don't stop now," I said. "Go on."

She took a breath and suddenly coiled and lunged at the next cart. At the same time Joey yanked the rope and he and the people in the rear seat all grabbed her as she crumpled into the front seat of the cart. I leaned as she lunged, and with her weight suddenly removed, my cart lurched. I had nothing to grab, and bounced down into the seat, my upper torso actually leaning out over the side of the cart where I caught a good glimpse of a hundred feet of air and a not-so-soft landing below. I closed my eyes and grasped, catching only air, and my feet slipped.

I was going over.

Then my hand hit something solid and I gripped it with every ounce of my strength. My other hand found it too, and my mind prayed, and after what seemed like an eternity I was able to open my eyes.

I was looking up, from outside my cart. One leg was wedged under the shoulder harness, the other dangled, and my hands gripped the edge of the fiberglass. Joey was shouting, others were screaming, but I was oblivious to it. Inside my cart, Rachel smiled and beckoned me to get in. Then she became Sally.

To this day, I don't know what it was, but it felt as if something grabbed my dangling leg and hoisted it into the cart, back to safety, and the image of Sally faded away. Then Joey was talking to me, telling me to put the rope on. I shook, trying to regain my breath.

I'd always questioned the validity of death-bed and jailhouse conversions; not that they can't happen, just that I doubted God worked that way. Yes, the thief on the cross was saved. But his response was not born of a hope for pardon and not just of a desire to avoid hell. He recognized Jesus for who He was, and asked to be remembered when Christ entered His kingdom. Fear of death or hell is not the basis for salvation.

Nor do I give any credence to those who, when faced with imminent death, make a vow to give their lives to God if He will spare them. God is not Monty Hall on *Let's Make a Deal.*

Why all this ran through my mind just then, I'm not sure. I guess it's because I knew at that moment what it felt like to face death and knew what prompted people who had rejected the Gospel all their lives to suddenly ask God to have mercy on their souls.

"Here it comes, Mr. Beckman!" Joey shouted. The rope flew over the back of the cart. I took it and fitted it around my waist, turning around gingerly in my seat so I was looking up. Trish shook and sobbed in the second cart, hunkering down so she was barely visible.

"Okay, Joey. Here I come." I stepped onto the seat, grabbing whatever I could to pull myself up. My arms ached and I realized I'd been tensing my whole body since we first crashed.

"Dear Lord, give me strength," I prayed out loud. My mother used to say that a lot, although I believe she said it for a different reason.

"What'd you say?" Joey asked. A news helicopter had flown over and began to hover, making it difficult for us to hear each other.

"I was praying!"

"Oh. Well, go ahead! Just don't stop holding on!"

I grabbed the back of the cart and stepped against the safety bar — hoping I didn't slip off — and drew myself up with my arms as I pushed with my right leg. It shook from the combination of adrenaline and terror, and as I looked into the faces of the other riders my

52

tenuous situation was even more revealed. Here I was, goodness knows how high, with nothing below me and only a rope that I'd knotted myself acting as my umbilical tether, trusting the instructions of a nineteen-year-old rehabilitating juvenile delinquent who hadn't particularly liked me since I arrested him a couple of years back. It was a situation I didn't really want to think about right then.

I brought my left leg up, found a foothold, and pulled myself up again, bringing the right leg up this time. By now I was on the back of the cart and could see down between the rails. Joey was standing on a steel rail, holding the other end of the rope.

I had two options: climb into the cart with Trish or stand on the rail with Joey. Okay, three: I could also plummet. I chose the first one.

"I'm gonna go for it," I told Joey.

"I'm ready."

I tensed my legs and sprang toward the cart, pushing off from mine. I landed heavily, raking my shins over the safety bar and causing all the carts to move, but they held, and I was in. Battered, bruised, and terrified but safe. Nerves were beyond frazzled, and several comments were thrown about concerning my having disrupted everything when I landed, but cooler heads told the complainers to shut up. For once, I said nothing. I was busy thanking God and promising to attend more Bible studies.

Trish was oblivious, crying softly to herself from her balled-up position next to me. I patted her shoulder. She startled a little but didn't acknowledge me. I told her it would be over soon, just in case she was still tuned in a little. To my surprise, she nodded.

Some of the people behind us cried or whimpered, others shouted encouragement, most just murmured to each other. One or two seemed to be enjoying themselves, at least now that most of the danger was over. One man complained about how long this was taking. The designer of the Dragon — the Dragon Master his coworkers called him — was silent, staring past me into space. He had deep ridges between his eyebrows and a pasty pallor that spoke of a fear greater than his current predicament: More than his life, he feared a flaw in the ride that might cost him his career.

"We need to release the damaged cart so the rest of them can be winched down to the hook and ladder," Joey said.

"Okay." Fighting nausea and dizziness, I held on to the safety bar and leaned forward to look at the kingpin. It was horribly twisted and didn't look as if it would release easily.

"Got a plan?" I asked.

"Yeah. They sent up a torch with me. As soon as it's clear below, I'm gonna cut it off."

I ventured a peek over the side. Security officers had already made sure no one was in the danger zone. One of Mr. Ozawa's landscaped areas was doomed, however.

"It's clear!" I shouted to Joey.

"Okay!"

The helicopter finally moved away. I heard the small, handheld torch click on and the gas hiss, then the scratching of the striker and a *fwoom* as Joey ignited the gas. In a couple minutes he shouted a warning, and, with the whine of stressed metal, the front cart that Trish and I had occupied moments before shifted downward and slowly gave in to gravity, toppling over the edge of the rail and plummeting silently to the ground. It landed with a sickening crunch, somewhat muffled by the foliage of the landing zone but collapsing on itself into a maelstrom of fiberglass and metal. Trish flinched when it hit but seemed to know the significance of it and visibly relaxed afterward. Her breathing slowed.

The release of the front cart allowed the rest of them — with us aboard — to roll forward a bit until the cable holding us went taut again. Total travel was less than a foot, but the jerky stop grated on raw nerves stirring a new torrent of fear and crying from those already so inclined, some sharp intakes of breath, a muffled scream, anticipating a resumption of our freefall down the track.

But the cable held.

The growing crowd of onlookers reacted with confusion to the plummet and landing of the car: the new arrivals gasping in horror, not knowing the cart was empty; the more seasoned spectators giving Joey a lackluster round of applause for his performance in climbing up and cutting it free.

Joey now gave the sign to employees below, prompting the distant whine of electric motors. We began to move slowly, steadily, and in a couple minutes we had arrived at the place in the track where the fire department ladder truck was waiting. A grinning firefighter stood at the top, ready to help us down.

"Okay, folks, just relax. We're going to take you down one at a time. You'll be fine, it'll be just a few more minutes. Anybody injured badly, think they can't walk down?"

"This guy's got a cut on his head but we stopped the bleeding," someone toward the center said. The fireman acknowledged them.

"She's pretty hys— shook up," I said, motioning discreetly toward Trish with a single movement of my head. I looked closer at the fireman. "Say, aren't you Russ Lefferts?"

"Yeah. How'd you know?"

"Besides your name tag, you mean?" He grinned at himself, and I said, "Wendy was always flashing your picture around. I'm Gil Beckman, from security."

"Oh, yeah. I've heard of you."

"How is she?"

"Oh, she's —"

"Maybe you two can have a reunion later," a woman behind me bellowed.

I waved to let her know I heard and turned to pry Trish's hands off the safety bar. She wouldn't budge so Russ stepped into the cart and told me to climb on down, that he'd take care of her. I hated to leave her but had to admit, I couldn't always be the hero. Sometimes there were people handy who could actually do a better job than Gil Beckman.

This ordeal was not over. We still had to conquer the ladder. The toughest step would be the first, from the cart to the ladder, and my legs were more than a little unsteady from the abundance of adrenaline my brain had pumped into them to prepare me for fight or flight, neither of which had been possible. Another fireman marked my hesitation and raced up to steady me, but by the time he was halfway up, I had made it and was on the way down. He retreated to receive me at the bottom.

Once I began to feel secure in my descent, I hazarded a glance over my left shoulder and saw a crowd of men gathering around the wreckage of our cart, trying to locate all the pieces. I shuddered.

There in the flower bed was one mystery, one puzzle, I wasn't going to be able to solve. I freely admit total ignorance of structural engineering. More power to them. I preferred human mysteries — voyages into the criminal mind, dark excursions through the damaged psyches of dysfunctional-familied sociopaths. Limits of adhesion and rolling friction computations are no less foreign to me than if they'd been written in Japanese. I get more out of watching Spanish-language sitcoms than I do out of the *Shadetree Mechanic* show. At least with the sitcoms, I know when to laugh.

I also saw Joey as he made his way — unhindered by a safety rope — down the superstructure of the Dragon, climbing quickly without a misstep until he was able to drop the last few feet safely onto the grass, to be congratulated and have his back slapped by his coworkers and cheered by the crowd. Cameras clicked and whirred as the newspaper and television folks descended upon him, breaking past the outnumbered and hapless security officers.

I felt rather sheepish as I was helped off the fire truck, in light of Joey's skill and derring-do. Nobody else cared, but it bugged me. I'd never been any good at climbing — six-foot walls gave me a run for my money — and I wasn't on a first-name basis with heights. As I touched the pavement, my knees buckled, and I leaned back to collapse onto the running board of the hook-and-ladder.

"Thank you, Lord," I prayed out loud.

As I rubbed my face I felt a hand on my shoulder and looked up into the face of Sally Foster, Security Chief Harry Clark's secretary and a very special lady to me. Tears streamed down her face as I stood up, taking her into my arms.

"It's okay," I said. "It's over."

"I thought I'd lost you," she breathed in my ear for no one else to hear. That said it all.

Next down was Trish, and I was surprised she was able to do it. Russ was a step below her, his arms on the rails by her side, guiding her down slowly, one step at a time. Occasionally he would place a hand on her lower back, just to let her know he was there. When she landed, Sally took her in but was unable to hold her up. Ambulance attendants moved in and packed her onto a gurney while Sally kept a hold of her hand. Actually, it was the other way around, with Trish holding Sally in a death grip.

In this manner, everyone was finally removed from the broken ride and brought to the safety of terra firma. Minor wounds were treated by paramedics, victims hugged and congratulated one another, and harsh words spoken during the crisis were forgotten. When the carts were empty a ride maintenance employee scampered up the ladder and released the cable from the rear cart. Because the track arced from down to up at this point, like a smile, the string of carts rolled forward gently, stopped, then rolled back again, repeating this until all momentum was spent and the string came to rest at the nadir. Tomorrow, a crane would lift them off one at a time, after they were separated from each other.

Trish and one other rider were loaded into the ambulance and taken to the hospital to be patched up. Television crews captured all the excitement of them being put in the ambulance and the door closing behind them, having missed getting footage of Joey climbing up or one ex-cop (and current fraidy-cat) hanging from the damaged cart from the top of the Empire State roller coaster, unless the helicopter managed to catch something on tape. Sally was driven to the hospital by Harry Clark, she to be with Trish, he to attend to his official duties as security chief and safety manager — such as finding evidence with which to place blame and taking the employees' statements to be used against them later.

As Sally sat in his electric cart (which would take them to his car), I leaned over and gave her an impromptu kiss, which she accepted readily, much to Harry's displeasure. He frowned upon public displays of affection by on-duty employees and would frown again later when the clip was shown during the news report — the proverbial *film at eleven* — but he said nothing.

A wise move on his part.

I managed to avoid most of the reporters ("What was it like up there?" one dope asked me. "Really high," I told him and turned away as he grumbled). I waded through the crowd to the men surrounding the catapulted cart. Security had reestablished a perimeter, assisted by firemen and local cops, and my former coworkers congratulated me as they let me through. For surviving, I guess. I hadn't done much else.

I sidled up to Dave Whelan as he pondered the offending set of wheels. He squatted to get a closer look, not yet seeing me.

"What do you think?" I prodded.

"Huh?" he said, turning to see who had interrupted his trance. The look on his face was the same one on the designer's when we were still four stories high. "Oh, it's you."

"Who were you expecting?"

"Opperman, naturally."

"Don't worry about him. He probably doesn't even know anything's happened yet."

Whelan didn't smile. He wasn't in the mood and I couldn't say I blamed him. The look on Dave's face changed as a realization came to him.

"You know, I'm sorry, Gil. I had no way of knowing this was going to break down. I feel terrible." He shook his head as he continued without a pause. "It was tested and tested and tested some more. There's absolutely no reason for it to have overstressed there." He pointed to a piece of twisted metal near what had been the right front wheel of the cart, the wheel that had jumped the track.

I patted Whelan on the back. He'd weathered two storms this past year — the death of one of his ride operators and theft of gold bullion from the museum by one of his maintenance men who was due to be tried shortly for it and for a ten-year-old murder — but this one was likely to be his undoing: He'd approved live riders on a roller coaster ahead of schedule, and it had ended in near-disaster.

"Nobody blames you, Dave," I assured. "It wasn't your idea."

"Yeah, but I should have said no. It's just that it had run flawlessly up until that time."

"Did the weight of the riders make a difference?"

Dave shook his head, not so much in a negative response but in confusion. "I don't know. Shouldn't have."

"We were the first added weight to go up, right?"

"The first people. We tested it with dummies —"

"Oh, you had management go for a ride?"

This cracked a smile on his lined face, but it was brief. "No. Crash dummies, just like the automobile manufacturers. We did it for several days running last week. In fact, we completely filled the ride. There was less weight today than then."

"Then that can't be it," I concluded, my simple mind capable of reaching broad conclusions with little information easily. Like I've always said, if something couldn't have

63

happened a certain way, then it probably didn't. To Whelan I said, "There must be some other reason why it broke, and it was just coincidental that it happened when we were in it. Something must've gone bad or been weakened but stayed put until we got on to push it over the edge."

I looked closely at the wheel set, called a truck, like railroad wheel sets. A boxcar has two trucks, each having two axles and four wheels.

"What's this do?" I pointed to the piece Whelan believed had given out.

"The primary wheels ride on top of the rail," he explained, "but a secondary set extends inside and below the rail, and when the carts are upside down they become the primary wheels."

"Is there any play?" I asked. "I mean, do all the wheels touch all the time?"

"Oh, yes, of course. If they didn't there'd be more bumping and jerking than a topless bar —"

"I wouldn't know," I assured him.

"No, of course not. What's more, though, there'd be more stress on that part if there was play, having to support all that weight without help."

"Could there have been play in this one setup? Maybe it worked loose or something."

"I don't see how, but we'll try to reconstruct it. The metal's so distorted it might be impossible to tell."

Although I'd decided earlier not to worry about what had happened, about what had caused the accident, I couldn't help myself, and Whelan didn't seem to mind. Maybe he felt he owed me something for almost killing me. I examined the piece closely, wiping a black powdery substance off the damaged metal right at the break with the tip of my finger. I rubbed it with my thumb and smelled it.

"You use graphite as a lubricant?" I asked.

"Yes, among other things. But not there." He leaned over to see why I asked. "What's that?"

"I don't know. Smell it."

He shook his head. "That's not graphite. It smells . . . burnt."

"I'm not absolutely certain," I admitted, "but I think it's the kind of residue left over after a small explosion. Like smoke and gunpowder residue."

Whelan's eyebrows bunched together in puzzled confusion, then raised over widened eyes as the implication unwound in his troubled brain. I wanted to avoid being overly dramatic, so I continued talking to keep from stringing him along.

"I'm not sure, Dave, but that's what it looks and feels like. It'll take proper analysis by the crime lab to pin it down."

"Crime lab?"

"Of course, Dave. Look over there. See that little silver thing? That looks like duct tape. You use that on your ride for anything?"

"No."

The closer I looked, the more I saw.

"And that. See there?" I pointed to a small, crumpled piece of plastic. "What's that?"

"I don't know."

"Neither do I, but I think it has something to do with a homemade bomb. Dave, if there was an explosive of some kind attached to your ride, someone had to stick it there."

"But what for?"

I chuckled silently. Was Dave in denial, or what?

"It's obvious, Dave. They were trying to blow it up."

"You mean they were trying to kill someone?"

"Not necessarily. They probably didn't know anyone was going to be on the ride. I think we have to assume, for the time being at least, it was the ride itself they were after, although people who do that kind of thing usually don't care if people are injured, as long as their objectives are achieved."

"Sabotage?" He said it almost reverently. "Like a terrorist thing?"

I shrugged, not wanting to commit.

Whelan leaned against the support pillar and grabbed his forehead. I didn't know if he was thinking or crying. I conducted a quick survey of the area. The people who do this kind of thing also like to watch their handiwork. Child abductors often volunteer to help with the search or to hand out fliers. They were here, I thought, or had been when I heard the pop just before we crashed, which I now believed was the explosive going off. They had been watching.

And once again, it had to be an employee. It was a question of access, motive, target, and expertise. The cops would have to be called in. I gave Dave some instructions and hailed one of the blue suits who had responded with the fire department and was still hanging around, talking to an attractive female employee.

I smiled inwardly. Maybe I'd get to swim in someone's psyche after all.

Four

A half hour had passed since the rescue. Trish and one other person were being held overnight for observation. Although not physically injured, Trish had been sedated because she was so traumatized. Sally was going to stay with her, at least until the evening.

Joey saw me inside the Dragon breakroom where I'd gone to get a cup of coffee and have a sit. I nodded to him. He dropped some coins in the candy machine and sat down with me to enjoy his candy bar, propping both feet on the table. He was looking pretty cocky, but I couldn't blame him. He was the media darling for his daring (that is, reckless and stupid) ascent up the superstructure to rescue us — with no safety harness or anything — and had been interviewed by all the networks and would be seen across the country by millions of couch-ridden Americans before the stroke of midnight.

More free publicity for the park.

I called Lt. Theo Brown, my ex-partner in

homicide, from the pay phone in the break-room. He said he was on his way, that he'd already heard about the rescue. Joey listened, his expression souring as he heard me tell Theo it had not been an accident. His chewing, however, was unaffected. Typical teenager.

I hung up and returned to the table.

"I owe you, kid."

"Owe me what?"

"My life, man. Me and Trish, and maybe everyone else, too. If you hadn't climbed up there like a fool, we'd be goners."

"Yeah, I guess," he said, matter-of-factly. He thought about it. "I suppose you're right."

Maybe this kid had some redeeming qualities after all, although that was a little difficult to reconcile when I thought about his other antics: burglary and vandalism.

"Where'd you learn to do that?" I asked.

"Do what?"

"Climb. Don't tell me you've never climbed before. You did it too easily. Weren't you scared?"

He shook his head. "Nah. Did you know that a fall from twenty feet is just as deadly as a fall from two hundred? Or two thousand? The key is knowing how to climb, and not think about falling. The more worried you are about falling, the more likely you are to fall."

"I'll remember that," I said, "the next time I stand on a chair to change a lightbulb. Which is about as high as I ever want to go under my own power."

"Weren't you on the S.W.A.T. team?"

"Yeah. In my youth."

"Then you learned to rappel, right?"

"Yeah. It was part of the training. But that was just sliding down a rope. The worst that can happen is the rope breaks, and that's highly unlikely. Besides, you weren't using a rope today. Your safety depended on your grip. So, where'd you learn?"

"You're not going to like it."

"Probably not. Go ahead."

"From climbing up freeway signs and overpasses —"

"To tag," I finished. Graffiti. The more difficult the target, the more acclaim delivered by their peers. Several kids had died locally during the past year trying to spray paint the center divider on the freeway. One tried to paint the end of a moving bus. The front end. Taggers are not the most intelligent of God's creation. I told Joey, "It's too bad you can't channel that knowledge and skill into something useful. Or at least legal."

"Today was legal."

70

"Yeah, it was. But what about tomorrow? I mean, you getting the job drawing Everett cartoons might satisfy your craving to create and draw, but what about your desire for climbing? I hear that really gets into the blood. The need for more height, more dangerous obstacles, more impossible . . . say, why don't you get into rock climbing?"

"You mean like Mt. Everest?"

"No, not that kind. I mean like that stuff they do now with just their bare hands and tennis shoes. Like what you did today, only on granite. Maybe when we get off work we can go to the sporting goods store. They've got the equipment, books . . . everything you'd need."

"Uh . . . well, maybe I'll look into it sometime."

"Whatever," I shrugged. "Just an idea."

"Yeah. I'll think about it."

"Okay." I paused for an awkward second, trying to think of something to say, but quickly gave up. "Well, anyway, I've got to go out there and wait for the police. Thanks again, Joey. And I really mean it."

"No problem," he said, and I left.

I joined Dave Whelan on the lawn near the smashed cart. A uniformed security officer stood next to it, keeping the curious away

— people like Jerry Opperman, the park's eccentric president, who was berating Whelan as I approached. Opperman's face was red, his arms animated, his words moist, as he made his position perfectly clear.

Whelan just stood there taking it, absorbing the abuse. The Dragon, although the concept had been suggested by Everett Curran in his plan, was completely under the direction of Opperman. This was the only new ride that he had much of a hand in, and he was making the most of it. He still felt threatened by Everett, by the young man's genius. That Everett was dead didn't assuage Opperman. The Plan lived on and would have done so without Jerry. He was afraid the owners would realize he wasn't a necessary part of the equation any longer.

I'd known it for a long time. Most everyone else did, too — except the owners. They were effectively insulated from the knowledge that Opperman was worthless and gave him all the credit for every success — which he humbly accepted without reservation — and his underlings took responsibility for every failure.

That's because that's what they were fed by Opperman. They accepted his reports as truth, interested only in the bottom line: profit. As long as there was a profit, they were quite satisfied to believe anything he told them.

Unfortunately for Jerry, the Plan didn't contain much with his stamp on it. He managed to wrest control of the roller coaster and told his boy in D. and P. to make it happen. Which, to his credit, he did. And now success was suddenly jeopardized, on the eve of the big opening, no less. It could be Jerry's ruination . . . we hoped.

But he's one of those guys who can make chocolate frosting out of mud. Not that it tastes like chocolate frosting; he just has a knack for making simple-minded people think it does and fearful people say it does. The publicity spawned by the crash would only be bad if it had been because of a design flaw, which it wasn't, so neither Jerry nor the park were likely to be hurt by it. But that didn't put a damper on Jerry's fury.

He was laying into Dave Whelan as if Dave had personally made sure the ride would break. Apparently he hadn't explained to Opperman that it was sabotage, or Jerry hadn't been listening. No, it's more likely Jerry hadn't given him a chance to explain. That's how he was when he was mad, so totally focused on himself and his little problems that he was uninfluenced by the facts. Shoot, he didn't listen when he was in a good mood; when he was happy he was in another galaxy. Right now the park president was so scared and upset that he couldn't be rational if his life depended upon it. He had probably started yelling before he even got there.

"Excuse me," I said. Neither of them had noticed me, and even now I remained unacknowledged. I said it again, louder. "Excuse me, Mr. Opperman!"

"Huh?" He swirled around, almost toppling over. "What?"

I let him recognize me before I answered. "There's something you should know."

"And what might that be, Mr. Buckner?"

I was making progress. At least he was in the ballpark. Two syllables and it started with a B.

"This wasn't Dave's fault." I said. "Or Design and Planning's."

"And what do you know about it? You're just a security guard." Apparently he was still having trouble getting used to my reassignment.

"I was on it, Mr. Opperman. I was up there when it happened." I pointed to the highest part of the track. "And besides, I haven't been a security guard for a year. And what if I was still a security guard, for that matter? I didn't spend fifteen years as a cop for nothing." I'd had it up to here with Opperman.

"For your information, Jerry, there's no problem with the design. I hate to admit it, but it's a good ride."

Opperman's expression relaxed. "What are you saying?"

"I'm saying — and Dave would have told you this if you'd let him — that it was no accident and wasn't the result of a design flaw. The ride was sabotaged. Someone meant for that to happen."

Opperman looked off over my shoulder, then back over his own at the fallen cart.

"Someone's trying to ruin me?" he asked quizzically.

"I hadn't actually thought about it in quite those terms," I said, considering the idea, "but I suppose that's a viable possibility." I hoped it wasn't the reason — too many suspects. "It's an avenue I'll look into."

"You?"

"Lieutenant Brown, I mean. And speaking of Lieutenant Brown, here he is now." I almost hated to admit to Opperman that his ride wasn't a failure, that someone had for whatever reason — tried to scuttle it. But truth is truth, no matter how unpleasant it might be. And the ride was a good one . . . if you like coasters.

"See here, Lieutenant," Opperman began as soon as Theo was within earshot. "Mr.

Breckman here —"

"Beckman," I corrected.

"— tells me someone purposefully tried to sabotage my roller coaster."

"They didn't try," I said. "They succeeded."

"I suggest you make haste here," Opperman went on. "There's a madman on the loose."

Theo was laconic. He took a final drag on his cancer stick, flicked it casually onto the grass, and blew the smoke more or less in Opperman's direction, although he feigned trying to direct it away while catching the breeze just right.

"Good afternoon, Mr. Opperman," he said. "Were you addressing me?"

"He was just thanking you for coming," I said.

"Ah, yes." Theo nodded. "Yes, of course. My pleasure. Gil tells me your ride broke, and it may have been other than an accident."

"There's no doubt!" Opperman huffed. "This ride was perfect! Someone . . . well, someone did something to it. They made it break!"

"How bad are the injured?" Theo asked, looking at me.

"Not too. Cuts and bumps, mostly. Trish

is pretty shaken emotionally. They're keeping her overnight for observation."

"Trish Smith?"

"Yep."

"Hmmm. And you say you were on it too, huh?"

"Uh huh."

"What'd you see or hear?"

"Well, these things make a lot of noise, you know. But I heard a distinct pop just before we left the track. There's some sort of soot on the part that broke, looks to me like powder burns or flash burns. Maybe smoke residue, similar to the halo on the end of the cylinder of a revolver that's been fired."

"Where are they? The damaged pieces, I mean."

"Right where they landed." I pointed them out. Theo sauntered over and gave them the once-over, jotted a few notes in his pocket notebook, then unfolded his cellular phone and made a call.

"Forensics will be here in a few minutes," he told me as he snapped the phone back together.

"Look here," Opperman protested. "Is this going to delay the opening?"

"Is the track damaged?" Theo asked, not ignoring Opperman but not answering him directly, either.

"We don't know yet," Dave Whelan said quickly, sensing Opperman's preparedness to give a premature and uninformed blessing to the integrity of the structure.

Theo looked at Whelan expectantly, not knowing him.

"Dave Whelan," I introduced. "Head of Rides. Dave, Lieutenant Brown."

They shook hands.

"Lieutenant Brown," Whelan mused thoughtfully. "Didn't you solve the case a few months ago where the girl's remains were found under the Starcoaster?"

Theo smiled but didn't say yes or no. He gave me a smirk that Whelan mistook for humble assent and continued his questioning.

"When will you inspect it?"

"As soon as we get a crew fitted up and some equipment inside," Whelan explained. "We'll probably wait until the park is closed to do it, though. It'd be too big a mess to haul that stuff in here with a crowd like this. Do you think there'll be anything wrong?"

"You tell me. It looks like there was a small explosive on that wheel set. The nature of the charge I can't say yet —"

"Can't say, or don't know?" I asked, for clarification.

"Both. I can't say because I don't know.

78

It wasn't much explosive, though, just enough to stress the parts or cause a malfunction, not enough to blow the thing to the moon. Gravity and kinetic energy would — and did, apparently — do the rest."

Theo lit another cigarette. "Even if the explosive didn't damage the track, losing that cart might have. You probably ought to go over it with a fine-tooth comb, check for stress fractures, dings, scraped paint, anything that could indicate a possible problem."

Opperman snorted. "We know our business quite well, thank you. We'll do our job and you do yours . . . and do so quickly, please."

"We're not going to go through this again, are we?" Theo asked, irritated. "I thought this was settled last time. We have a crime scene here, and we'll take all the time we need to process it."

"Crime scene? No, we have an accident — a misfortunate scene. And even if someone did sabotage me here, this is an internal problem. You're here at our request. In fact, I don't recall giving the order to call you, now that you mention it."

"I didn't mention it," Theo said dryly.

"Didn't need your order," I told Opperman. He looked at me like I'd just passed gas. "The park is not the only victim here. You know, sir, with all due respect, I'm getting tired of your silly posturing and self-interest." I could see Dave Whelan's eyes widen. I continued undaunted. "I know you're trying to protect the park's interests, not to mention your own, but sweeping things under the rug and interfering with a criminal investigation doesn't accomplish your objectives."

Opperman tried to interject. "And just who —"

"I'm not done, Jerry." I held up my hand. "I care about the park, too, but I care about the people who work here as much or more than the park in general. The reality is, this park is nothing without the people who work here. This is more than just a slight accident on a roller coaster. Lives could have been lost today. It's only by the grace of God they weren't. You need to wake up, sir. Someone here is trying to ruin the park, and in doing so they came close to killing a bunch of people." I held my thumb and index finger an inch apart to show him how close they came. "And since I'm one of those people, that makes me the victim of a crime. As such, I called the police, and right now Lieutenant Brown is the best friend you've got, because whoever did this may try it again. Now stop trying to get in his way."

There was a strained silence in our little group until a maintenance worker standing at the fringe began clapping slowly. He was soon joined by others, and, although I waved them off exaggeratedly, Opperman scowled and slunk off without comment.

"I wouldn't want to be you right now," Dave Whelan muttered when Opperman was out of earshot.

I shrugged. I wasn't pleased with myself, but it had to be said. Opperman had been getting in the way long enough. I'd go talk to him later, see if I could smooth the creases. I doubted it, but as a Christian I had an obligation to try.

Actually, a few years back I would have just told him to stuff it and get out of the way. Maybe I was mellowing in my old age.

I know what the Bible says about being a good employee. Frankly, that's what I was being. I had the interests of the park and its employees at heart — listen to me, the quintessential company man — but I felt that Jerry Opperman didn't. If he owned the park, it would be a different story. But he was an employee, just like the rest of us, albeit with a larger paycheck and a really neat chair. And what's right is right. Occasionally Christians need to stand up for truth even if there's risk involved.

Despite the fact that I disliked Jerry — on several layers and for several reasons — I still wasn't sure I was right in saying it. Not that I was wrong in *what* I said, but for having said it. Maybe I was having second thoughts because I was afraid of losing my job.

Oh well. What's done was done. I shrugged it off as I watched the forensic guys arrive and set up shop. Mr. Ozawa, the landscaper, appeared and began hovering and fussing, concerned about the damage to his flower bed and hoping the feet of the cops wouldn't make it worse. Which they did.

With nothing left for me to do here but get in the way, I nodded good-bye to Theo and left to retire to my office and think about how to approach Jerry . . . and what kind of job I should look for next.

The situation called for dinner at Hollie's Hut. But that would have to wait until later. Right now I had to get a cup of employee cafeteria coffee and do something to solidify the jelly still lingering in my knees. The excitement was catching up to me, and my harangue to Opperman didn't help. Once I relaxed I'd try to talk to him, then grab a quick bite to eat before heading over to the

82

hospital to visit Trish.

I hoped Sally would still be there. I needed her moral support, not to mention whatever sympathy I could coax out of her.

Five

"Yes? May I — oh, Mr. Beckman! Please come in. What can I do for you?"

Elizabeth Potter, Jerry's ancient secretary, smiled up at me from behind her desk. She was typing on her computer, and, although she looked up and greeted me, her fingers didn't stop flittering over the keyboard. I noticed with a glance how arthritic those fingers were and wondered how she could manage to type so quickly and without any apparent effort. Surely she must be in pain.

"How are you doing, Mrs. Potter?"

"I can't complain," she said. "I've been better, but I've been worse. How about yourself?" She finally stopped typing.

"Oh, I'm fine, considering."

"Your little adventure today?"

"You heard."

"Who hasn't? When the phone call came in, Jerry rushed out with fear scrunching up his face. When he returned, he was brighter than a beet. So I called around and found out what happened."

"Is he in?"

"Yes, but I'm not so sure you should go in just now."

"He's busy with someone?"

"Hardly. He's in a mood. Worse than usual. When he came in he was muttering your name. Or something close to your name, that is. Didn't even acknowledge me — not that he ever does — and slammed his office door behind him. He even adjusted his chair."

"How do you know that?"

She grinned sheepishly. "I could hear it whirring and humming through the crack in the door. He even turned on the massager. That was over an hour ago."

"Maybe he's dead," I suggested. "Vibrated his heart into arrhythmia."

"No such luck," Mrs. Potter lamented under her breath. "I'll announce you, if you want. Though I really don't recommend going in. Maybe tomorrow."

"Do you really think he'll be different by tomorrow?"

"No," she sighed. "You know, Gil, I sure miss Mr. Golden."

"From what you've told me about him, I can understand that. Things made a lot more sense when he was here, so I've heard. He died about three years before I got here, but I've been told by a lot of people how much better it was."

"Don't get the wrong idea," Mrs. Potter cautioned. "He wasn't perfect. He had his quirky eccentricities, too. Like not hiring certain minorities until the laws forced him to, and promoting only from within as a reward for being here a long time, whether or not they were qualified. Everyone started at the bottom, regardless of experience. On the plus side, Mr. Golden was loyal to all his employees, and those who stayed were treated well. Too good, in fact. We've got a couple old timers —" She smiled. "Other than myself, I mean — who are on the dole. They do nothing and get paid handsomely to do it, but that's part of the Golden legacy that was left intact. I daresay that type of thing will stop when those folks are finally gone."

"Too bad," I said. "I was going to ask how I could get one of those positions."

"You couldn't sit around and do nothing. It's not in your blood."

"I guess. Tell me something, Mrs. Potter, if you don't mind."

"Why do I stay on when I could retire at a good salary?"

I smiled and nodded.

"Because I love this place. I like working here. I like the people — most of them, at least — and I have nothing else to do. I'm

86

like you, Gil. I have to stay busy. There is no Mr. Potter anymore. He died ten years ago. Oh, don't look so sour. The last five years of his life he was a total pain." She laughed heartily. "I loved the man dearly, but facts is facts. I'm married to the park, and this is where I'll stay — Jerry or no Jerry. I like to do my part to keep it running like Mr. Golden would have wanted it. It's not easy, what with the owners' group making the major decisions as a committee — you know how that works — and Mr. Opperman with his. . . ." She trailed off, apparently yielding to the maxim to not say anything if she couldn't say something nice.

"I understand," I said.

"Don't get me wrong," she said. "He's got his good points. Some of his ideas are okay, too. And he usually lets me do things my way, the way Mr. Golden would have done them. He recognizes my importance here, my link with the past. But the truth is, he's not an administrator. His talents are better suited elsewhere."

"A common problem here," I observed.

"Yes, to be sure. But not uncommon with any large organization. What can you do when there are so many people making decisions with no real lines of communication and little accountability? That's his biggest downfall. He should be coordinating every-thing, not hiding out in his office playing with his chair." She blushed. "I've said too much. You sure have a way of getting people to open up to you. Must be your police training or something."

"Nah, I just have that way with women," I bragged. "They want to tell me their deep-est secrets, then they shake my hand, tell me they're grateful I let them get that off their chests, and fall in love with someone else. All my life I've been a big brother."

"That's not a bad thing," Mrs. Potter said, "if women feel comfortable around you. I've seen that assistant of yours — Trish, is it? She adores you. And Sally! Now there's one you won't lose to someone else if you play your cards right. Just hang in there, Gil."

"Sally is special," I said dreamily. "And thank you for your candor. Truth is, I was beginning to think maybe I was all wet in my assessments, that Opperman was a genius, the park was being run properly, and I was just an ignorant ex-cop who ought to keep his nose clean and his mouth shut."

"Well, that's good advice, anyway, Gil. Just remember, it's going to take more than just one person's opinion to change things around here. And the reality is, it may never change. We have to learn to live with it. Are you religious, Mr. Beckman?"

"That depends on your definition, I suppose. In the sense that the world defines it, I guess you could say I am. But I'm not religious for religion's sake. I'm a Christian. I go to church and fellowship with other believers. I don't smoke and I don't chew, and I don't go with the girls who do."

Mrs. Potter chuckled heartily. "I haven't heard that in a long time. Well, since you're a believer, you know that God wants us to be content, no matter what situation we find ourselves in."

"I've been dealing with that this past year," I admitted. "I haven't been too good at it."

"You left the police department prematurely, I understand." I nodded and shrugged, wondering if there was anyone at the park who didn't know. She went on. "Sally and I have done some serious talking. No, don't look at me like that. Sally and I have been friends for years. We met at a Bible Study Fellowship meeting. She's like a daughter to me. She thinks the world of you, Gil, but she's concerned. She told me about your wife and how she died. I can imagine how upsetting that would be. Did that have anything to do with your quitting? No, don't answer. Just think about it. But if it did, you need to reevaluate yourself, for Sally's sake as well as your own."

She paused mercifully to let that sink in, then said something that nearly bowled me over.

"Your wife couldn't have children, could she?"

Stunned, I could only shake my head. How did she know? I wondered. I might as well have said it out loud for she answered me.

"Maybe she died of a broken heart, Gil. I don't know. Or maybe God didn't give her children because He knew she wouldn't be around to take care of them."

"Sh-she lost two," I stammered, unable to keep it back, my eyes suddenly clouded and burning. Mrs. Potter got up and padded over to me, then gave me a big hug.

"Poor dear," she said quietly, breaking off. "But we have a big God. We don't have to run from our problems or hide behind false fronts like this whole park does," she swept her arm toward the amusement park. "Nor do we have to mope around, trying to fathom the way God works, or living in the past, or squandering the rest of our lives because something happened we don't understand. You do your job here, obey God's Word, and you'll be fine. And if God means for you and Sally to be together, don't let the memory of your wife destroy that. Accept God's gift, thank Him, and do your best to love her. And if He opens the door to return to the police department, don't look back. He gave you the talent and abilities you have." She sat down in her chair. Court was apparently adjourned.

"I've said too much," she concluded. "If you really want to see Jerry, go ahead. But I think it'd be better to let him get over it and talk to him tomorrow."

I nodded, still unable to say much, then thanked her and left. I had gone in there to talk to Jerry, to explain why I'd said what I had out at the ride, and left after coming face-to-face with my own fears and inadequacies. Not quite what I had in mind.

But Mrs. Potter was right. It was painful hearing it, but I knew I probably wouldn't have listened to anyone else.

It was five o'clock. I left the park without returning to my office, deciding against going to Hollie's Hut before I checked in on Trish at the hospital. Besides, Sally was there, too. And I needed some emotional support.

Harry looked tired. No, he looked worried. Not concerned, although I'm sure he was, but worried, self-indulgent. No one was injured badly enough to crease Harry's forehead like a paper fan from a Chinatown trinket shop. Events like this have a way of folding the foreheads of managers. Dave Whelan, Harry Clark, Jerry Opperman . . . all of them would be pacing their offices in the morning, their heads down, looking as if they'd run into the same accordian and contemplating how this incident could spill over and get them wet.

You could never tell where the backlash could go. It would snap back like a steel cable under tension that breaks, taking out everyone in its path without prediction and without prejudice. Like God, runaway cables and other major snafus are no respecter of persons.

Yet managers are resilient. If the cause had turned out to be employee error, they'd find something wrong with his trainer, or the training itself, then fire the employee, the person who trained him and his supervisor, even if the training orders originally came from themselves.

In other cultures, managers are the ones who toss people into volcanoes.

Harry's problem was an obvious breach in security. Somebody had planted a bomb. If it was an outsider, Harry might be history; an employee perpetrator would be only slightly less damaging to the security chief.

But that's what I thought it to be: another

employee gone off the deep end. The park was beginning to resemble the post office.

It had to be an employee. Who else would have had access to the ride and been able to plant the explosive? While possibly unavoidable — who could forsee something like this? — this was the third major event in a year, and Harry was unlikely to escape completely unscathed. Under his nose, so to speak, an employee had been murdered and another had stolen two hundred thousand in gold bullion. Now this. Harry's only salvation might come by blame-shifting or creating a diversion. I reminded myself to watch my back.

Harry was in the hospital lobby when I entered, but, although he was looking right at me, he didn't react.

"How's it going, Harry?" I asked quietly, with respect.

"Not good, Gil."

"Is someone worse off than we thought?"

"Huh? Oh, no, nothing like that. Everyone's okay. The Smith girl is sedated. She's not injured. It's just to make sure the shock didn't do anything to her heart, you know."

"Yeah. Overnight observation."

"And everyone else was treated and released, except Amy Scattamachia."

"The wardrobe designer?"

"Uh huh. She's got a concussion, and they noticed a little problem with her ticker. A little irregularity. She's in her room, hooked up to a monitor."

"So what are you doing hanging around here?" I asked.

He glanced around as if taking in his surroundings to get his bearings, then he thought for a second. "Oh," he said presently, "I'm waiting for Sally. She's in with Trish, keeping her calm. She'll need a ride."

"I can handle that," I offered. "You go on, I'm sure you've got a lot to do."

"Thanks, I — listen, I'm sorry. How are you doing?"

"Oh, I'm fine. A little shook up but none the worse for the wear."

"Well, I understand you did a good job up there."

"I didn't do anything but survive. Joey Duncan is the hero. Did you see the way he climbed up there?"

"As a matter of fact I did, and we're none too happy about it."

"Who's 'we'?"

"Me, for one. And Jerry. And our insurance people, when they find out about it."

"He saved lives, Harry."

"Yeah, well . . . maybe. Who knows what would have happened if he'd waited for the fire department? It might have ended the same."

"And the whole string of cars might have gone over the edge if he hadn't tied us off. I agree, it was a risky thing. And I'd probably have stopped him if I'd had a chance. But since it turned out okay, I suggest we leave it be. Besides, what are the chances of it happening again? He no longer works for Rides; he's a cartoonist. And I've got to tell you, he looked like he knew what he was doing."

"Where'd he learn it?"

I smiled. "You know kids." I left it at that. "Frankly, I think the park would be well-advised to give him some official recognition . . . but I guess it's not for me to say." I shut up after that. I was learning.

Harry gave his shoes a serious study, then said, "Well, I've got to get back." He reached out to shake my hand. "See you tomorrow, Gil. We'll talk about it in the morning. I'm sure you're exhausted after all that."

As I grasped his hand I said, "Michelle says you want to talk to me about Eric Hiromoto." Harry's hand was clammy and wet. When we let go, I casually put mine in my pocket to wipe it off.

Harry gave me a blank look for a response, trying to remember, then his face relaxed.

"Oh, yeah. Right. We'll talk about that to-morrow, too. Shoot, I don't know what this is going to do to their visit."

"What do you mean? Do you think Hiro-moto will cancel out?"

"No, but —"

"You're afraid he'll change his mind about the whole deal."

"No . . . no, not that. It just doesn't look good."

"Things like this happen, he knows that. I'm sure he's had problems in his businesses. Besides, it wasn't an accident. You know that."

Harry nodded. "Why'd they do it?" he asked, almost pleading for an answer. "Do you think it had anything to do with Hiro-moto?"

"Heck if I know," I shrugged, employing the strongest word in my vocabulary to help convey my total lack of insight. "Doesn't make any sense to me. If that's the case, why do it before he gets here? Why would making the ride crash — and maybe killing someone — change Hiromoto's mind about the business deal? And isn't he, like, a real old guy? What is he, seventy? He wouldn't even be getting on the Dragon, so that can't be it."

"What about one of the people on the ride

. . . even you? Could someone else have been the target?"

I thought about it. "No. I don't see how. Us getting on the ride was a last-second thing. Besides, why endanger so many people when you're only after one?"

"To make sure you get the one," Harry said, proving he had learned something during his police career. "Or to make it more difficult to discover who the intended victim was, because if the victim was easily identifiable the suspect probably would be, too. Still, since, as you say, it was a last-second decision. . . ."

I raised my eyebrows and curled up one corner of my mouth. "You got me, then. I don't have a clue. But I'm sure Lieutenant Brown will figure it out."

"I hope he does it quickly. I'd like to have a lid on this by Saturday." He looked at his watch. "Uh oh. I've got to go. So, you'll take care of —"

"Sally? Sure. We've got a dinner date anyway."

A look of chagrin flashed across Harry's face. He was none too pleased about his private secretary dating one of his subordinates. I couldn't blame him, really, but he had nothing to be concerned about. She wouldn't tell me any of his secrets and I wouldn't ask, and since our relationship was only casual — in the sense that there was no pillow talk, and we seldom were even alone in each other's house — well, like I said, Harry had nothing to be concerned about. His secrets were safe.

It wasn't that anyone believed Sally and I weren't being intimate. People have a tendency to judge what others do based upon what they would do in similar circumstances. And since most previously married adults in a dating relationship would be indulging in mutual gratification, people at the park who knew we were seeing each other naturally assumed we were dallying.

Not much I could do about it, except to avoid circumstances that could set wagging tongues in motion.

Harry bid me good night, and I watched him plod out of the hospital, his thick-soled shoes clumping on the pavement, his stooped shoulders swaying back and forth as his stubby arms flopped, hanging loosely at his sides as he walked without pumping.

I obtained Trish's room number from information and made my way up to it, not really thinking of anything in particular. I involuntarily recalled being up in the damaged cart, hanging over the abyss, and forced myself to concentrate on something else lest

I get weak-kneed at the realization of just how close I came. Not that death is such a bad, or even scary, thing. And although I was prepared to go, I wasn't ready, you know what I mean? If Christ took me home, I wouldn't complain, but as long as I was here I still had some things to do.

Like eat dinner, I thought as my stomach moaned. Like Paul, I was ready to buffet my body, with a silent "t."

The Christian credo: Do nothing to excess, but when it comes to food, get as close to excess as you can.

The elevator *pinged*, and the door opened. I stepped off, turned to the right as the sign directed, and found Trish's room. Sally was seated in a chair by the bed, holding Trish's hand, and patting or rubbing it occasionally. We exchanged smiles before Sally put her finger to her lips.

Trish was asleep. Sally carefully set the sleeping girl's hand on the bed, adjusted the covers, and we left the room.

Out in the hall I asked how Trish was doing.

"She'll be okay, but she was really freaked out. She's led a pretty pampered life. Until last year when Everett was killed, she'd hardly known adversity. With wealthy parents, raised in a Christian environment but without much in the way of needs, her only friends the kids from church, where her family spent a good deal of its time. . . . She's never had to really face her own mortality."

I nodded, but didn't say anything. What I was thinking was that even the most life-experienced person, those who have dealt with death on a regular basis or have been in shootouts or fights, or worked the streets in a gang-infested inner city . . . none of that makes looking down death's throat any easier when the time comes, especially in a situation where you can't fight or shoot your way out of it. Gravity just doesn't fight fair.

Courage, which is what Sally was really talking about — and what Trish lacked — is not an absence of fear, but moving ahead toward one's goal or task in spite of one's fears. For the Christian, it also means trusting God more than circumstances. Anyone who has no fear is emotionally dead and would also have no compassion or joy or love — and no sense. Fear is the emotional equivalent of pain, which lets you know something is wrong and should be dealt with. Fear is an indicator, a warning signal, to let us know there is danger.

But I said none of this to Sally. If she wanted to think I hadn't been afraid, that was okay by me. The fact is, I was scared to death. I've just learned over the years to function without letting it get the best of me.

She put her hand through the crook of my arm.

"I'm glad you're okay," she said. "I can't tell you how worried I was when the call came in that you were stuck up there."

"Ah, come on," I urged. "Try. Tell me how worried you were."

She patted me playfully with her free hand but didn't release her grip. "You're too big-headed as it is."

I smiled.

"You ready for Hollie's home cooking?" I said as we stepped off the elevator.

"I think it would be better if we go to her restaurant," Sally said.

"That's what I meant."

"I know. That was a joke. Don't you know sarcasm when you hear it?"

"Not unless it's coming from me."

"Well, I'm famished," Sally admitted. "Oh, by the way, I called the Currans from the waiting room in E.R., told them about what happened. They wanted to come down, but I told them she was out of it. They said fine. They'll pick her up tomorrow."

"Good thinking. And I'm glad you remembered our date. To be honest, it completely slipped my mind until a few minutes ago

101

when I smelled the cafeteria food and realized how hungry I was."

"My poor baby."

Sally took my hand. I crossed the parking lot, trying valiantly to act nonchalant with a goofy look on my face.

"So, how's the lovebirds?"

Hollie came toward us smiling as we entered her restaurant.

"They're fine," I said. "We left them at home with the cockatiel and the parakeet twins."

"I mean you guys, silly," Hollie chided.

"We're fine," Sally said. "And you?"

"Oh, I'm great, honey. When you-know-who goes to the john, I'll tell you about this guy I'm seeing."

"Can't I listen?" I asked, feigning hurt feelings.

"No," both ladies said at once, and they laughed.

"It's none of your business," Hollie said. "Come on, your table awaits."

"What else would it be doing?" I queried but was soundly ignored.

We settled in and a pot of coffee was brought by Jose. Hollie poured it herself, then patted me on the arm and grinned. "She's a keeper," Hollie said softly, then winked at

Sally. "So's he." Then she left us alone.

"She certainly got over me fast," I said, trying to sound disappointed.

"Oh, yes," Sally deadpanned. "She's rebounding so hard you could play her off the back wall." Sally wasn't sarcastic as a rule, but that was the second one tonight, and I laughed.

We ordered and ate, conversing all the while, and had a thoroughly enjoyable evening together. I didn't want it to end but was really tired after my busy day and near-death experience — the only thing missing was a bright light at the end of a tunnel and wispy angels flittering about the place — so we skipped dessert, and I took Sally back to the employee parking lot at the park so she could pick up her car.

I parked by her car, shut off the engine, and jumped out to go around and open her door. She waited patiently and let me take her hand to help her down, then we walked hand-in-hand to her Toyota. In the moonlight, with the sounds and smells of the amusement park wafting over to us, I leaned over and gave her a slow, easy kiss.

"I'm so relieved you're all right," she said softly when we parted. "I would have been . . . very upset if you'd been hurt. You sure you're okay?"

"Yeah, I'm fine. I'll probably go right to sleep. After I get home, I mean."

"Okay, Gil. Good night. Sweet dreams."

I gazed at her, gave her one last kiss, and got back in my van as she drove away.

And after cranking the starter on the behemoth until the battery wore out, I had the mobile security officer on perimeter patrol call a tow truck for me.

Why is it that a fresh dose of reality always punctuates an otherwise beautiful evening?

Six

The next morning, after catching a ride to work with Joey, I lounged in Michelle's office. She'd left a message on my machine to see her first thing. While she spoke with her secretary in the other room, I drank her coffee and devoured a fresh blueberry muffin. She had one on her desk, too — I'd brought them with me — but hadn't touched hers. In fact, once I thought about it, I realized I'd never seen her eat. Maybe she viewed eating as something to be done in private. Or perhaps watching me had ruined her appetite.

Then again, maybe she ate like a troll and didn't want to tarnish her image.

Fat chance. I had to admire her decorum. Even on the hottest days she didn't perspire. Her hair was never out of place, and she always looked as if she'd just gotten finished getting ready, even at the end of the day. She was straight out of one of those old television commercials for hair spray. You remember those.

And, when things were bleak or the day hadn't gone well, Michelle still had a ready

105

smile and her temperament was always balanced, under control. With her natural beauty — classic Asian features and perfect skin and teeth — I had to wonder why her husband divorced her.

But he was Japanese, wasn't he? Not an American of Japanese descent, but a Japanese national. I imagined he was pretty traditional in his outlook, and having a wife who was a high-ranking official in a large business might not sit well with him. And there was always the possibility that her demeanor at home was not the same as it was here. Maybe she was a grouch, or. . . .

Nah. No way. That couldn't be it. Well, I'd probably never know. And Theo wouldn't divulge anything. He'd tell me to pound sand.

"Gil!" Michelle said sharply, breaking into my thoughts.

"Huh?"

"Where have you been?"

"What do you mean?"

"You were in outer space somewhere. I thought maybe you'd gone to sleep, except you were still chewing and your eyes were open."

"Sorry. I was just thinking about something."

"What?"

"Well . . . I . . . I was wondering how you're able to look so good all the time, and always have a happy disposition, and how you put up with Jerry Opperman's non-sense."

"*Giri,*" she said, sitting down and pushing her muffin off to the side.

"What's that?" I asked. "Some kind of food supplement?"

She laughed. "No, you're thinking of *gin-seng.*"

"Oh, yeah. That little root thing in the bottle."

"*Giri* is something my mother taught me. I can't explain it. Look, I've got something important to talk to you about."

Uh oh, I thought. *This does not bode well.*

"I . . . I had a talk with the owners yester-day . . . just before the accident, in fact."

"Yeah?"

"They said they thought we were progress-ing just fine on the makeover of the park, and Design and Planning was up to speed now. Most of the blueprints are done, and it's just a matter of scheduling to get the new rides and upgrades going. With Everett the Dinosaur now a fixture here, the cartoon strip taking off and everything else. . . ."

I could see where she was going but she was taking an awfully long time getting there.

I sensed her discomfort, although I didn't know exactly why she felt it, but I thought I'd help her through it.

"I'm laid off, is that what you're trying to tell me?" Although not surprised by this turn of events, since my current position was temporary from the start, I was nonetheless a little surprised that it was coming so soon. Jerry must've been really incensed. My stomach did an acid dump, and my head began to get woozy.

"No, no," she answered quickly. "Not at all. It's just that your assignment is, they feel, at an end, and they think you should resume your former duties. In fact, I understand they are preparing some sort of bonus to show you their appreciation."

"So I'm back in uniform," I sighed with resignation. "When does this take effect?"

"You go back to security next month. You and Harry can discuss the details, but I doubt he'll put you back in uniform. I suggested he find something more suitable for your talents."

"Well, thank you, but I don't believe security has a Grand Vizier." She laughed a little, in spite of herself, seeming almost relieved that I wasn't ripping her office apart. I went on. "What about pay? I suppose that will go back down to previous levels?" That's the problem with temporary assignments that come with a pay raise: sooner or later you lose it, just when you become accustomed to the income. Fortunately, I hadn't increased my debts, but I needed to. The thousand dollars I'd put into my van only extended its life a few months, and it was living on borrowed time.

"I'm sorry," Michelle said quietly, leaving my assumption unconfirmed or denied. I could tell by the compassion in her voice as she gazed at me that her sorrow was genuine.

Taking a quick breath, I found a smile down deep and exhaled it. "Thanks. I'm sorry too. But, hey! I knew it would happen sometime. It was fun while it lasted; it was certainly more than I expected or deserved —"

"I wouldn't say that," she countered.

"I don't have any complaints. Any legitimate ones, that is." I glanced at my watch, more a gimmick than a need to see the time, since a large plastic Everett the Dinosaur in his time machine with a digital clock on the side of the contraption adorned the wall behind her head. "Oh, I've got to run."

As I stood to excuse myself, her phone rang. She answered it, listened for a few seconds, and a severe look creased her normally smooth face. Her eyes locked on mine in horror.

"The armored truck is being robbed!"

"Who? Where?"

"Two men, main gate." She repeated the information the caller had given her.

I was on my feet and headed toward the door. "Are there any — what kind of weapons do they have?" I had started to ask if they had any weapons, immediately realizing no one in their right mind would rob an armored truck without them.

"Guns."

Big surprise, but that's all the caller knew. That's all people ever see, and I had to admit, I couldn't blame them. They see a gun, a big gun. Always a big gun. When you're looking down the barrel, they're all big.

I was out the door and running.

The park bank was located by the main gate, and once a day an armored truck arrived to remove excess cash. That had to be what she was talking about.

The park was crowded, this being a holiday week, which would be both good and bad for the robbers. Good because there would be more money to steal; bad because there would be more witnesses.

Just what I hoped to accomplish by going there I wasn't sure — unless it was just to be a good witness. Perhaps I could get a license plate number, a physical description, recognize a physical anomaly on one of the perps that the average, untrained citizen might miss, like a scar on his arm or a nervous tick, or even that he was left-handed. I was definitely not preparing to confront them. I had been denied a concealed weapons permit, thanks to Captain Fitzgerald, so a direct encounter was not on my agenda.

While pushing my way through the teeming masses of funseekers — ignoring their verbal abuse at my haste — I ran the possibilities of what I'd find through my mind, to prepare myself for any eventuality.

Officers spend their free moments, such as when driving around on open patrol, going over in their minds different scenarios they might one day face — a felony car stop, a robbery at a certain location, that kind of thing — so that when the event actually occurs, they will respond in a predictable and appropriate fashion. Several years back I was critical of the way an officer responded to a shooting — he had hid rather than taking cover and returning fire — and I was told my criticism was unwarranted, that nobody knows how they will respond to a situation until it happens. I disagreed, telling them that under those circumstances I knew ex-

111

actly how I would respond. The way it had gone down was likely to happen — the car the officer was chasing stopped and everyone bailed out and began firing — and I had visualized that exact scenario hundreds of times over fifteen years in the field. Right or wrong, successful or unsuccessful, I knew how I'd react. It was how I had conditioned myself. That's what range training is all about. Studies have shown that cops will function under stress exactly how they operate on the range. If they pick up their expended brass after every string of fire, they will be in a shootout picking up their brass. If they reload standing up on the range, they will reload standing up in a real situation rather than taking cover.

And so, as I hurried to the main gate, I visualized what I'd do and how I'd react. The bank is an underground facility, accessible only by a key-entry door inside the park near the main entry gate. The door opens directly to an elevator and a staircase, one on the right, one on the left. Both require a second key. Once downstairs you're in a small, bare lobby with another door into the bank, but there is a thick, glass window with a small port at the bottom through which bank employees do their business.

This is not a bank in the consumer sense.

It serves only to collect and count all money coming in and leaving the park. No one goes in — even to the downstairs lobby at the window — except bank employees. They pick up the money from all areas of the park periodically during the day, take it in small hand trucks under armed guard — off-duty police officers in street clothes — and turn it over with recap sheets at the window, never going inside. Only those who count the money are allowed inside.

The only time there is even a risk of robbery is when the armored transport arrives. It does so once or twice a day, usually at a scheduled time but occasionally when requested by the bank as warranted by unexpected revenues. Upon arrival it backs up to the main gate and the guard gets out and meets the employee, completing the transfer.

That thirty seconds — from the time the bank employee exits, walks to the main gate, hands the money to the guard, who then walks ten feet or so to his truck and tosses it in — is the critical period. That's when the money and the people are the most vulnerable. It is then that would-be robbers are most likely to strike. After that, the armored vehicle is secure and on the road, and even if accosted, would not likely be within sight of park employees.

Assuming Michelle had been called sometime immediately following that thirty seconds, I was already a good two minutes late
— the time it took me to traverse the park
on foot — and the whole event would be
over, the robbers having already made their
escape.

I was surprised, then, to find the robbery
not only still in progress but chaos of major
proportions. People inside and out were still
scattering. There were whimpers and crying
from frightened children, the armored car
was still outside the gate, and two people —
a guard and a hooded civilian — lay motion-
less on the pavement near the truck.

I strained to assess what had happened. I
hadn't heard any shots, but that didn't mean
anything. They could have been fired before
I left Michelle's office or been overwhelmed
by the park's usual noises. The reality is,
though, that guns don't sound in real life as
they do in the movies. They *pop,* surprisingly
quiet. *Kablam!* is Hollywood sound effects.
A backfiring car is generally louder than a
handgun. And with the screaming of guests
on rides, the steam whistles, roller coasters,
Western town gunfights, a couple of pops
out here would probably not be heard except
by people watching the robbery unfold. And
if someone else did hear it, they wouldn't

give it a second thought.

I even realized there were probably a few people who thought this was part of the entertainment, and these folks were dangerous. They might decide to walk right through it all, thinking it's all part of the show.

The downed guard's breathing was shallow, and he did not stir. The other man, dressed in dark clothing with a ski mask over his face, showed no signs of life at this distance. What was happening? Were there others? Surely no one would attempt this kind of robbery alone. Perhaps his accomplices had fled. How many were there? If they were gone, why was no one attending to the injured guard?

No, there were still bad guys here, somewhere.

Ah yes, a brown Cadillac in the taxi zone out front. I could see it, some fifty yards outside the main gate. Apparently unoccupied but not to be taken for granted. It had that "getaway car" look all over it.

Sirens in the distance. Moving clouds passing in front of the sun, enough to erase any shadows. The main gate area clearing of guests and employees, inside the park and out. Muffled cries, a few screams, an angry shout to shut up. Scuffling feet.

I crouched behind a frozen-banana cart,

scanning the area for suspects. To my right, hiding between the rows of guest lockers, several families huddled with a couple of employees, the latter just teenagers. One, a red-headed female in the ragged cavewoman outfit of the main gate ticket-takers, I recognized. She was composed, trying to soothe a distraught woman and her hysterical children. I caught her eye and motioned her over. Without hesitation she said something to the mother and crouch-walked to my position, ducking down next to me.

Even in the stress of the situation, I couldn't help but notice her brilliant, thick, shoulder-length tresses, freckled nose and petite yet attractive figure, accentuated by the rough-cut fur outfit. She smelled of . . . shoot, I didn't know what it was, but it definitely was not Au de Woolly Mammoth. A slight sheen of perspiration had broken out on her temples. Although composed, I could see now that her hands shook. As she squatted next to me, she lost her balance, and I instinctively put my arm around her waist to steady her.

"Thanks, Mr. Beckman," she said with great respect for her elder, bursting my bubble instantly and launching me back to my senses. "I'm okay now."

"Did you see what happened?" I asked as

I removed my arm, and she changed her footing to a more stable position.

"Yes. I was at the reentry gate as usual and happened to be watching as the armored truck backed in, and the guard got out. It all happened so fast." Her breathing became audible and fast.

"Okay, take it easy. How many are there? Suspects, I mean."

"Three. One of them got shot by the guard. Actually they shot each other at the same time. Oh, this is so terrible! I hope he's going to be okay. The guard, I mean. And I think there's another guard still in the truck. One robber is inside."

"Inside what?"

"The park. He dragged Brian off with him."

"Brian?"

"Yeah. He works for the bank."

"He was the one bringing the money out."

"Yeah."

"Where's the money and the other suspect?"

"Brian threw the money on the roof of Guest Relations. See?"

I could indeed. A large canvas sack, full of who-knew-how-much cash — possibly half a million or more in small bills — resting on the edge of the tiled roof.

"So Brian came out with the bag . . . then what?"

"He was about to open the gate to hand the bag to the guard when the two men came running up waving guns and shouting. The guard turned and pulled his gun out and they both fired, then they both fell down. The other guy forced his way through the gate, but Brian had already tossed the bag up. The robber saw it and knocked him down, then dragged him off into the park, that way."

She pointed to the other side of a landscaped area, in front of which sat a scale model of the revisions to the park, including Moonraiders and the Dragon.

"So where's the third guy?"

"He was still in the car when it started. I don't know now."

As I stared toward the Cadillac in the taxi zone my question was answered. With the sirens drawing nearer a head popped up in the suspect vehicle. The guy looked around wildly, shouted, "Benny!" a couple times frantically, then started the car, peeling out down the access road to the public street.

Two down and one to go.

I got the description of the remaining suspect from the cave girl then said, "Rita, go to the pay phone by the lockers, dial 911 and give the police the description and direction

118

of travel of that car."

"Yes sir, Mr. Beckman," she said. She jumped up immediately and disappeared into the lockers.

Security officers were converging on the scene. I hailed the closest one, filling him in quickly on the suspect and his last known location. The officer radioed his counterparts and directed them to keep people out of the danger zone, to block off the paths — not an easy task with this many guests and such a large area, and made especially difficult when we weren't certain where the suspect had gone.

Then another guard called to report he had sighted the suspect holding Brian at the edge of the landscaping where no one could circle behind him within sight of the main gate. That was about twenty-five yards away, but around a slight bend that kept us from seeing him . . . and him from seeing us.

A muffled voice to the rear spun us both around, and we were suddenly confronted by a seven-foot gray dinosaur, an apatasaur on his hind legs to be precise, its pear-shaped body supporting an egg-shaped head. Everett's mouth gaped open in a permanent and delighted grin. Behind the black mesh were two human eyes we couldn't see, eyes belonging to the occupant of the costume.

"What's happening?" the dinosaur said without moving his lips in a cracking adolescent voice, muted by the outfit.

"Get back!" I ordered in a stage whisper. "What are you doing here, Everett?"

"I dunno," the boy inside said, shrugging as best he could in the costume. "I just suited up, and they sent me to work. Is there something going on?"

"Yeah, a robbery."

"Whoa, I'm outta here!"

I had an idea, a crazy one. We needed to get closer to the suspect but without endangering anyone. The arrival of the police was imminent, and they had no idea what they were getting into. With two wounded people lying outside, they might rush up and become targets.

"Wait a sec!" I said, grabbing his big, soft arm. "Take it off."

"Take what off?"

"The costume. What else?"

"Right here? In front of everybody?"

"It's an emergency. What's the matter, you naked in there?"

"No."

"Then do it!" I doffed my suit coat and tie as the bewildered kid pulled off the head.

"I'll need help," he said.

I undid the velcro in the back, and he

quickly stepped out of the top half of the suit.

The design of the costume was an innovation. Normally, character costumes like this are made for really small people, no more than five-two or three, and they are hot and heavy. This dinosaur was in three parts — legs, body and head — and could be worn by male or female, five-foot to six-three. The secret was the legs. They were chest high trousers with suspenders, like fishing waders, the body having two holes in the bottom for the legs to fit through, thereby making it adjustable for height. That Everett might one day have short legs, the next day long, was inconsequential and unnoticed by most. The head was light, about a pound, made from molded expanding polyfoam around a bicycle helmet.

The kid had it completely off in a minute. I stepped into the pants, the body, then strapped on the head as the velcro on the back of the costume was pressed into place. The top of the neck was velcro'd to a ridge around the base of the head, completing the costuming. My view through the mouth was limited, but it would have to do.

"Can I get my hands out somehow?" I asked the lanky teenager.

"Yeah," he said, still puzzled about the goings-on but not questioning me. "On the

121

inside of each wrist there's a slit. Yeah, right there. Just pull it open and out pops your hand."

I was in business. Almost.

"Hey, Muldaur — oh, there you are," I said to the security officer with me. "Do you still carry that .380 inside your shirt?"

"How did you —"

"Just give it to me."

He complied, somewhat hesitantly, and pleaded, "Don't tell anyone where you got it."

"Don't worry. It's only in case of an emergency. I trust it's ready to go? Round in the chamber? Full clip?"

He nodded, but I checked it anyway. When it comes to guns, never trust what someone else tells you. A mistake on their part could mean departing before the rapture on your part. I withdrew the gun into the dinosaur's arm and sealed it back up. "Talk about concealed," I mumbled.

"What's that?" Muldaur asked.

"Nothing. Thanks. Say, do me a favor, will you? Don't broadcast the disguise business yet, just in case the suspect is within earshot of someone's radio, okay? I need the element of surprise for this to work." To the kid from the costume I said, "Tell Rita on the phone over there to tell the police the dinosaur is an armed ex-cop. Got it?"

He nodded, grinning nervously, and ambled off toward Rita.

"What's your plan?" Muldaur asked.

I turned so I could see him through Everett's open mouth.

"Did you see *Jurassic Park?*"

"Yeah. Who didn't?"

"That's my plan."

Before he could question that, I waved good-bye and plodded out into the open just as several police cars slid to their individual stops outside, and the officers and detectives bailed out and took up positions of safety behind their vehicles. One car — no, two — peeled off and accelerated down the drive in the same direction as the suspects' Caddy.

I ignored the action outside the park, although it was clearly visible through the iron gates, and wandered across the open area, my new feet plopping on the painted asphalt. My movements were exaggerated, cartoonlike, as I strained to pinpoint the suspect.

Over the years I'd learned to dislike trying to communicate with anyone whose face or eyes I couldn't see — people wearing sunglasses, Halloween costumes, clowns, and especially people in character costumes.

Knowing there was a person inside was no comfort. They could be male, female, pretty, ugly, nice, mean, sick, sleepy . . . you just never knew. Without something to gauge them by — a face, a voice — they were amorphous, and for all practical purposes they became the character whose image they wore. That's good for an amusement park but bad when you're trying to communicate with them.

Furthermore, you could never tell what they were really thinking or doing in there. An eighteen-year-old in a dog suit can leer at women, even touch them in inappropriate places, and get away with it because, after all, it's just a cute cartoon-like dog. Little do they know it's a teenager with raging hormones.

John Wayne Gacy, the infamous serial killer, was well-known for dressing up as a clown and entertaining kids. He even bragged that clowns could grab ladies' behinds or other private areas and the women would only laugh, because, you see, it was a clown and just part of the joke. Ominously, he also said clowns could get away with murder.

That's why I hate costumed people. It's also exactly the reason I was inside the dinosaur now. It was the only way I could think of to "sneak up" on the suspect.

Trying my best to bounce along like Charlie Chaplin's Little Tramp, I scoured the bushes, hoping he hadn't moved or taken more people hostage. It had only been a few minutes, though it seemed longer. I could see the security officers keeping the crowds back in the distance, assisted by a few other brave employees.

There, off to my left, behind a low marquee announcing the day's special attractions and concealed by a fake rock and some bushes . . . yes, definite motion.

I stopped, turned to face him, and put my hands on my hips in an exaggerated motion. When he didn't respond, I clomped closer, pointing to him with a dinosaur arm and waving him out.

"Don't come any closer, you . . . whatever you are!" he shouted.

I cocked my head to one side then held my palms up in a questioning stance.

"I've got a gun!" he announced.

I pretended to shake, knocking my knees together. Poor Everett, the stupid dinosaur, thought it was an act, all part of the show. At least, I hoped that's what he'd think.

"Who is that creep?" I heard the suspect ask his hostage.

"It — it's Everett, the dinosaur," Brian's voice quivered. "H-he's the park mascot."

"Get him out of here, before I have to hurt him!"

"Go away, Everett!" Brian yelled.

I pretended not to hear, folding my arms and tapping my foot.

"Go on, Everett, get out of here!"

I didn't move.

"He doesn't want to," Brian told his captor, as if he was translating a foreign language.

The slime bucket gave it a try himself. "Go away you piece of —" He unleashed a torrent of profanity.

I stuck my fingers in my ears — well, in the sides of my head where ears would be if I had any — then held my arms out and wiggled my fingers.

"He won't go away till he gets a hug," Brian said. "That's the way he is. He hugs everybody. Especially women."

The robber grinned. "Sounds like a good job," he muttered. "But not now. Look, I don't want to hurt him, but I will if I have to."

"Maybe he doesn't understand," the kid explained. "Maybe he thinks this is just part of the show. Let me go give him a hug, and he'll go on." Then he added in a flash of brilliance. "He's deaf, you know."

The suspect pointed the gun at Brian's nose. "What do you mean, he's deaf?"

"Everett. He's deaf."

"That's ridiculous," he growled. "It's a person in a costume."

I had taken the opportunity to move closer, and when slime ball glared at me again I held my arms out and bounced up and down in happy anticipation.

"Please, mister," Brian begged. "They hired a deaf kid. He's a little slow, you know what I mean?" Brian pointed to his own head. "He loves kids; that's why they picked him. I won't run, I promise. Let me get Everett out of here."

"Go easy, kid," the gunman said through clenched teeth. "Two steps. If you make a break for it, Everett is one dead dinosaur."

I'd only been a dinosaur a couple minutes and was already near extinction.

Brian nodded. I'm sure he didn't have a clue what he was going to do, but I gathered he was thinking of running for it, hoping Everett could get away, too. As soon as he was close enough, I hailed him in a whisper the suspect couldn't hear.

"Stop, Brian, but don't react. That's good. I'm not the regular kid in here. Give me a hug just like you said but let me move toward you. When I give the word, you jump out of the way then take off. I'll take care of this guy." I clomped toward the kid and held my arms out, then gave him a big hug, twisting from side to side.

"That's enough!" the gunman shouted angrily. "Now get him out of here!"

I continued twisting to the right, then said, "Now!" and gave Brian a shove. At the same time I moved toward the gunman as my hands found their way out of the costume sleeves. As the surprised robber saw the automatic pistol in my human hand, he brought his gun up, but I had been anticipating that and was already reaching for it with my left hand. I grabbed his revolver from underneath around the cylinder so it couldn't be fired.

"No hug, huh?" I shouted, and at the same time twisted his gun upwards and towards him, wrenching it out of his hand. He shrieked at the sudden stab of pain in his trigger finger, which, unfortunately for him, was still engaged within the trigger guard. I raised a dinosaur foot and delivered a jurassic karate kick to his solar plexus, knocking him sprawling into the shrubbery, his gun now residing safely in my hand.

Brian waved the security officers in, and they swarmed the fallen suspect, while police officers, still a little bewildered at what they had witnessed, moved in with paramedics to see to the injured people outside the gate.

I drew the .380 back inside the sleeve, and, after dropping Muldaur's weapon into my pants pocket, did a little dinosaur victory dance. The cops streamed through the gate to take custody of the profanity-spewing suspect, and I noticed that guests and employees alike were converging on the scene with cameras clicking and whirring. Everett bowed, flexed his biceps, and when a familiar detective happened too close to collect the suspect's firearm, he found himself suddenly swaddled in a big dinosaur hug, just as a photographer from the local fishwrapper prepared to take a shot.

"Let go of me, you twerp!" the detective said, trying to peel me off.

"Ooh, Detective Manhandles Hero," I said, mocking a headline of the event. "Bad public relations."

Theo stopped struggling and strained to see into Everett's mouth. Cameras clicked.

"I know that voice," he asserted. "Gil, you get your behind out here where we can see you."

The crowd was thickening as word of the botched robbery spread, pressing in on the hasty perimeter set up by the blue suits.

"Not in front of all these fans, Lieutenant," I told him. "Especially the kids. It'll destroy the illusion." I raised my arms in victory, and the people responded with cheers and applause.

A radio squawked and a uniformed officer came up to Theo and whispered to him.

"Thanks," Theo said, and turned to me. "They caught the guy in the Cadillac."

"Good. How's the guard?"

"It didn't appear life-threatening. He got hit in the ten ring but was wearing a ballistic vest. He'll be bruised, but should be okay in a couple days. The bad guy didn't fare so well."

"Dead?"

"Like a cheap battery."

"Hey, he's one of God's children."

Theo smirked. "Was. And when did Gil Beckman get to be so compassionate?"

"I can't help it. It's the costume. It exudes compassion."

"Speaking of which — the costume, that is — I can't stand trying to talk to you in that. I can't see your face; makes me nervous. Go get out of it so we can get a good interview from you."

"Gladly. I never knew being a dinosaur could be so hot. You'd think they would have appreciated the ice age."

Seven

"So, anything new on the roller coaster tragedy?" Theo asked me when I'd finished giving him my version of the foiled robbery. Since I hadn't needed the gun I borrowed, I left that part out.

"Excuse me?" I said. "That's what I was going to ask you. You're the detective."

"You expect me to believe you haven't been doing some snooping around on your own?" I shook my head but he ignored me. "I know you, Gil. You can't help yourself. You're driven to investigate things. It's a passion — an addiction. It's a . . . compulsion with you!"

"Hold it!" I protested. "You're making me sound like I need to go to Detectives Anonymous. 'Hello, my name's Gil, and I'm a sleuthoholic.' For therapy they make them watch *Murder She Wrote* and turn it off halfway through. If they don't get the shakes, they're in remission."

Theo chuckled. "You couldn't quit if your life depended on it. If a mystery gets anywhere near you, you're going to try to solve it."

"Hey, I can quit any time I want to. . . . I just don't want to."

"That's what I thought. Now what have you found out? Surely you've at least got a theory."

We were relaxing in a breakroom, drinking vending machine coffee. "I told you — nothing. I haven't done a thing. I've barely had time even to think about it. Oh, Harry Clark and I did some speculating in the hospital waiting room last night, but we came up with zeroes. In fact, I assured him *you'd* get to the bottom of it quickly."

"Thanks for nothing. So what were those theories you bandied about?" He smiled smugly, still believing I'd done some checking around.

I just shrugged. "A lot of people could be affected by this. The designer, the builder, Rides Chief Dave Whelan, Harry, Jerry, Larry, Moe, and Curly . . . you'll have to come up with a victim on this one, probably, to understand who did it."

"What about the park itself as victim?"

"You mean to hurt it financially? Or discredit it in the public media? Yeah, that's a good possibility. But there's a whole covered wagonload of disgruntled ex- and current employees to sift through, many of whom have an axe to grind."

"How many of them are explosives knowledgeable? That would narrow it down some. Maybe Sally can do a background search for military vets."

"That might take awhile."

"That's fine. Could one of you on the ride when it crashed have been the intended victim?"

I shook my head. "No, I don't think so." I explained the circumstances under which we were on the ride.

"If no person was the target, then someone was trying to sabotage the ride. It's rather obvious."

I thought about that, and it seemed to be the only answer. "This is a big 'what if,' " I said slowly, "but what if it wasn't supposed to go off when it did?"

"What are you getting at?"

I took a sip of coffee, just to make him wait.

"I don't know what this means, really — what the implication is — but the charge had obviously been installed some time before it went off. What if it was supposed to be blown at a later date?"

"For what purpose?" Theo asked. He lit a cigarette but I pointed to the "No Smoking" sign on the wall. "Phooey," he said, but he didn't put it out. "Let's go outside, walk around."

"Good idea," I agreed. "Fresh air. People will probably be coming in anyway." I dropped my coffee cup into the receptacle and slipped on my coat.

Outside, we strolled through the Western town, Theo puffing contentedly.

"I thought you were going to quit," I observed.

"I never said that," he declared, taking a long draw.

"You never used to smoke. Not so much, anyway."

"No?" He flipped the butt onto the ground a few steps ahead of him then stepped on it as he passed by. As we left it in our wake a skinny Asian kid in white overalls with a buzz haircut, his name tag proclaiming him to be Joe, scooped it up with the broom and dustpan he carried.

"Okay, you don't want to talk about it," I said. "I'm just concerned about your health, that's all."

"Yeah, I know." He exhaled slowly, not a sigh, really, just a clearing of the lungs in a pensive, perhaps even melancholy way. But not a sigh. Irritation, maybe. Yeah, that's what it was.

"So I'm concerned," I said. "So sue me. Look, Theo, I can't help noticing the changes in you since you got promoted to lieutenant right after I left." I paused. "By the way, you have me to thank for that promotion. If I hadn't left —"

"I wouldn't have got promoted because you would have?" His tone was sardonic. He knew I was just trying to get a rise out of him. "You would have gone from detective straight to lieutenant, leapfrogging over sergeant? Well, we'll never know, will we, Gil?"

I grinned. "Oh, I know all right. I just can't prove it." He snorted and I continued. "Anyway, I'm a little surprised at how you've changed. I mean, I really noticed, not seeing you for a year until Everett Curran was murdered. I didn't say anything, but I'm really getting concerned. Is being a lieutenant that much more stressful than being a detective sergeant?"

"Yeah, it is, as a matter of fact. Before, we just had our caseloads to worry about and the lieutenant chewing on our behinds every day. Now I have to do the chewing, plus carry a caseload of my own —"

"All the heavy stuff?"

"Not all of it, just the high profile homicides — the one or two a year of those — and the P.R. stuff."

"Like keeping an eye on Michelle when her husband was acting up last year?"

Theo suppressed a grin. "Well, that was

kind of . . . my idea."

We arrived at the entrance to the Spine Tingler, another roller coaster that wasn't yet finished. This one was a lollapalooza. We're talking g-forces and zero gravity and tight loops and . . . well, you get the picture.

As we stopped to look at it, Theo continued.

"Now I've got to ride herd on a bunch of rookie detectives while Captain Fitzgerald breathes down my neck with his pompous attitude and ridiculous ideas and alcohol-tainted breath . . . the kind left over from the night before." Theo shook his head. "I smoke from stress."

"You need Christ," I said bluntly, surprising myself. My heart began to thump. It sort of just rolled off my tongue. I hadn't planned to witness to him. I'd known him a long time, had even discussed religion with him before, but always felt self-conscious about trying to disciple him.

I guess it was because he knew so much about me. He knew about my mistakes: the times I had slipped up and said something I shouldn't have; the times I let my eyes linger on a passing young lady; the bad decisions I'd made; my weaknesses . . . in short, Theo knew about my sins. I had messed up my life pretty good — at least *I* thought so after realizing I shouldn't have quit the department — and I sure couldn't use my life as an example of the benefits of Christianity.

Truth is, I didn't think there necessarily *were* humanistic benefits to becoming a Christian; at least, not tangible benefits the world expects. Putting your faith in Christ as Lord and Savior does not erase your debts, or get you a better job, or get you out of jail, or make your spouse stop beating you, or get you that new car you so richly deserve. Those things may not change one iota. What does change is where you'll spend eternity and who controls your life.

I fully expected a wave off, or a crack about how weird Christians are, or even a cordial, "That's okay for some people . . . maybe I'll look into it when I'm old."

But that's not what he said. What he did say caught me off guard.

"Yeah, you're probably right."

My response could only be described as . . . unrehearsed.

"IIuh?"

"I said you're probably right," Theo repeated slowly, clarifying it with fake sign language. "I've watched you the last year or so, and even though you goofed up pretty good by leaving the P.D., you seem to be in pretty good shape. Emotionally and psychologically, I mean. Your attitude's even improved."

What's that supposed to mean? I wondered. But I didn't ask. I didn't really want to know. Instead, I tried to put it in perspective for him.

"That's the working of the Holy Spirit. Look, Theo, I don't want to give you a whole course in basic theology —"

"And I don't want you to."

"What *do* you want, Theo? Let's start there."

"That's the point, Gil. I don't know. I just feel like there's . . . something missing."

I took a deep breath and thought a quick prayer for the right words. "God puts into every person an emptiness that only He can fill. Some try to fill the void with possessions, or work, or family, or sex, or drugs, or alcohol. Some even try to fill it with religion."

"What's wrong with religion?"

"God doesn't want us to replace love for Him with love of worship. Even the pursuit of religion is self-serving. Anyway, most people disregard God as the answer to their hollow lives until one day their conscience is seared and God closes the void, giving them over to their lusts. Others seek God, but not in the right way. They try to reach him by doing good works, or becoming active in

138

social or church programs, or they believe they can achieve God-consciousness by self-awareness or chanting or what have you."

"Okay, Gil, I'll bite. What's the only true way?"

"Just like I've told you before."

"I need Jesus." There was no unusual or mocking tone in Theo's voice.

"Well, yes, although that's rather a simplistic way of putting it. Having Christ in your life doesn't necessarily mean attending church, or giving money, or reading the Bible."

Theo looked a little surprised, but I held up my hand to stave off his questions. "I'll go into that some other time. What's important now is to understand what being a Christian really means. What say we grab some bench?"

I meandered through a scattered group of yakking, laughing guests toward a rustic park bench, actually the seat from an old buggy, still with its springs. The wood was so old it had been worn shiny and smooth. As we mounted the boardwalk, I looked around at the ghost town and wished that, for even just a few minutes, I could experience a real Western town: the sights, sounds and smells, the dust, the tinkling pianos, the horse liniment, the starched cotton calico dresses, leather saddles, homemade pies, gun oil, the classic *clip clop* of the prevailing mode of transportation. I didn't want a re-creation, I wanted the real thing.

As we settled onto the park bench, Theo checked his watch.

"I don't have much time, Gil, so make it quick."

"Okay, I'll give you the short version, but promise me you won't reject what I have to say based just on the highlights. Give me a chance sometime to go over it in depth."

"Just don't expect me to fall all over you believing it, either."

"I wouldn't want you to. Giving your life to Christ is not an impulsive thing. You're a detective, Theo. I expect you to withhold any decision until you've heard all the facts and had all your questions answered."

"Go ahead, then."

"Okay. Remember, this is all in the Bible. These aren't Gil's ideas, they're God's." Theo nodded his assent and I kept going. "We're all sinners, Theo. Every person on earth. Even the greatest religious leaders and the little old ladies. It's not just what we do that is sinful, it's what we think. There's no way we can keep from sinning. And even if someone could honestly say they had only committed one sin in their entire life, they're still condemned by it, because if we have broken one of God's laws we have broken them all. We all deserve judgment.

"But He wants us to be with Him, so He had to come up with a way of making it possible for people to be acceptable without violating His standards or His righteous judgment."

"Okay so far," Theo interrupted. "The penalty for sin had to be paid by someone."

"Right. Someone had to die in our place. But who was qualified? It couldn't be someone who deserved to die themselves; they wouldn't be doing anything but paying the penalty for their own sins. It had to be someone who didn't deserve to die, someone who was sinless."

"And that was Christ."

"Right. God Himself came to earth in human form, lived as we lived, was subject to all the trials and temptations we are — and then some — but did not sin. He did not deserve judgment. He gave Himself to die on the cross, to pay the penalty for all mankind."

"Okay, He died in our place. But what's the big deal about the resurrection?"

"He truly conquered sin — and death — in rising again to life. Because He resurrected Himself we know that He'll make good on

His promise to resurrect us. The Apostle Paul said that without the resurrection, our faith is in vain."

I took a breath, then continued when I saw the expectant look on Theo's face. "If Christ is the Son of God, as He claimed to be, and lived a perfect life, dying on the cross and rising from the dead to ascend into heaven, all of which He predicted, then what is there to reject? And if He did all that, then His claim to be the Messiah, and Lord, and Creator of the universe and equal with God — all that can be counted upon as true. And if you accept all that, then why wouldn't you want to turn your life over to Him? That, Theo, is the question; the most important question any of us will ever have to answer for ourselves. That is what you need to think on."

"You've given me plenty to consider," Theo said quietly, his face knotted in a slightly troubled stare. "Let me mull it over, and we'll talk some more about it later."

"Fair enough."

I exhaled slowly, emptying my lungs completely before taking another breath to calm myself, to expend some of the adrenaline that my brain had squirted into my veins. I dared not show my shaking hands, keeping them instead buried deep in my pants pockets.

Theo would think on it. He was that kind of man, logical and methodical and honest. That's what made him a good investigator. And if the Holy Spirit was calling him, Theo would get back to me.

Although I didn't let it show, I was excited, for I had shared my faith with someone I'd known for years. Yes, we'd talked before, but those discussions had been more cerebral, more academic than out of any desire on his part to make a change in his life.

But it had been different this time. Something was going on that made him suddenly interested in God as a person, not just an entity like a Zeus or a Thor. Theo had become acutely aware of a vacuum in his spirit.

I'd leave it up to Theo to tell me about it when he was ready. I knew he would. I'd trust God to win Theo Brown. Gil Beckman couldn't do that.

We sat in silence for a few minutes, me thinking about Theo and Theo probably thinking about his situation — and hopefully about what I'd told him. The smell of *churros* and hot popcorn wafted past us, and an involuntary stomach response alerted me to the fact I hadn't had lunch yet.

"Do you have time to get something to eat?" I asked. "They've got some great hot dogs down the path a little ways."

"Yeah, I suppose," Theo said, standing up. "My treat."

I must've been getting through to him. I'd never heard him offer to pay before.

We strolled over to the cart and got a couple dogs each — loading them up with all the trimmings — then sauntered over to the edge of the path near the lake to eat them and wash them down with cold sodas.

Leaning on the rustic wood railing, we watched small, toy boats, maybe two feet long or so, putt around a small lagoon below us. They were piloted from a nearby bank of controls by kids and adults who'd dropped a quarter for a few minutes of time at the radio controls.

"So anyway, what about the Dragon?" Theo said after a while.

"Huh?" Watching the silent watercraft was soothing, and I was deep in thought.

"Your theories on the accident," Theo repeated.

"Oh. Some accident." I shrugged. "Someone wanted to delay the opening of the ride, that's what I think. Or discredit the park or someone in it."

"Who? And why?"

"You find the answer to one question, you'll have the answer to the other."

"Big help you are."

"So what do you want from me?" I asked. "You told me last time Captain Fitzgerald doesn't want me nosing around department business."

"That never stopped you before."

I grinned.

"Besides," Theo continued, "I figure this isn't just department business."

"I agree with you, but I'm at a loss on this one. What'd forensics come up with?"

"Not much. My guess is a blasting cap was used, based on the small amount of explosives. There were some ceramic fragments, some tiny pieces of what looked like electronic components . . . you know, resistors and stuff. And pieces of the casings from some AA batteries, and a long silver tube. It was all strapped onto the cart with duct tape."

"What do you make of it?"

"Best we can figure, some critical bolts holding the wheelset on were weakened by the charge, then finally snapped because of the strain put on them by the extra weight of the people on board. That's the sound you heard."

"The weight of people?"

"No, funny guy, the bolts snapping."

"But they had weight on the ride before," I countered. "They used dummies, because they have to know how it will function with people on it. You know, crash test dummies. No, I'm sure that sound I heard wasn't metal snapping. It was the explosion . . . if that's the right word for it, since it was so small. Any evidence of a timing device?"

"None. When were the dummies used?"

"Day before."

"Were all the carts checked after that?"

"Probably. That's what the procedure would be, to check the carts afterward to see what effect the extra weight had."

"Are those the exact same carts? I mean, there's more than one set, aren't there?"

"Oh yeah, there are several sets. I'll check with Dave Whelan on that."

"Might be the explosive device was attached when that set of carts was in the shop."

"What would be the point of attaching the charge in the shop when they could just as easily have cut through a few bolts, or loosened them? Why go to all that trouble? I'll tell you why. They wanted to control when and where the accident happened."

"Okay, let's say you're right. Just for the sake of argument, of course."

"Of course."

"Why use just a blasting cap? There's a possibility it wouldn't do enough damage to make the thing crash. And even if it did, there's no telling where it would be when it finally gave way and crashed. As it turned out no one was killed. Looks to me like a really stupid suspect, or there's something we're missing."

"Maybe both."

"Who could have done it?"

"You mean that works here?"

"Yeah."

"Anyone with a little mechanical know-how, access to the ride or the service barn, access to explosives, no alibi for the time-frame, and who has an axe to grind."

"That narrows it down," Theo said. "Looks like we're back to printing out a list of employees who could have done the deed. Someone with ability and access. Some psychotic vet with munitions experience. What about motive?"

"There's only one that I can see," I said. "The ride itself was the target, for whatever reason."

"What about Hiromoto?"

"Michelle told you about him, huh? Why would someone want to kill him? And why do it here? And there's other problems with that theory. He wasn't on the ride when it went off, and at his age he isn't likely to be riding it anyway."

"Okay, I'll go along with you there. He's here to bankroll a replica of this park in Japan, isn't he?"

"Yeah."

"Maybe someone doesn't want that to happen, thinks a problem with the new ride would scare him off."

I pondered what he had said. The theory was plausible but didn't answer why they assaulted the ride with us on it. I said so to Theo.

"To make it more dramatic," Theo concluded. "The more innocents hurt or killed, the more attention they get in the media. Of course, it could be they didn't know you were on it," he surmised. "It was a last minute thing, after all, wasn't it?"

"That's for sure. I didn't know until they forced me onto it."

"In that case, there's always the possibility that you were the intended target, and whoever set you up had a death wish for themselves, since they were going on it too."

I shook my head. "A big *no way* on that one, Theo. Trish was the one who got me on the Dragon, and she had no way of knowing I was going to be there. I was just wandering around."

"Then it had to be the empty ride that was targeted, not a person," Theo mused thoughtfully. "So we're back where we started."

"Unless . . ." I said slowly, "unless it wasn't the actual event, but just a test."

"What are you getting at?"

"We were testing the ride, correct? Well, maybe the bad guy was just testing his bomb-making ability and didn't know we would be on it. If that's true —"

"If that's true, we don't have a clue. Besides, how would he be able to time it to go off at just the right moment?"

"He would have had to set it off by hand. With a remote switch." My eyes lit on the boats floating past us. "A remote controller. A radio control unit. With any R.C. unit, like an inexpensive hobby model for planes or cars, the suspect activates the receiver unit, which is mounted with the explosive, which activates a servo, which activates an ignition source, which sets off the blasting cap, all in a split second. Easily done and with readily available parts, except for the blasting cap. But they're not impossible to come by."

"And that would account for all the pieces we found, like the long silver tube —"

"Antenna."

"Right. Everything but the ceramic."

"What about a spark plug? Could that have been the ignition source?"

"Maybe, but there's a lot of resistance in a spark plug. I don't know if AA batteries could do it. Besides, the ceramic wasn't smooth like the outside of a spark plug. But I'll have the bomb squad guys check it out."

"If that's what happened," I said, "then whoever set it off had to have been there when it happened. And in line-of-sight for the R.C. controller to work. That would mean he was under the ride somewhere."

"But if it was just a test, like you say," Theo said, "then he would have known you guys were on the ride and. . . ." His face wrinkled up in frustration.

"Unless he couldn't see us."

"What do you mean?"

"He could have been out of sight of the loading dock, even though he was under the track, and not known anyone was on the ride."

"Where?"

"Anywhere close by. Did you guys check the bushes under the ride?"

"Pretty much. Of course, we weren't thinking about that angle, so we didn't go too far away from where the cart fell."

"You got a minute?" I asked.

"Lead the way."

While we hiked through the amusement park, dodging folks in shorts and tank tops and restraining each other from stopping at the caramel apple and popcorn carts, we shared our personal lives with each other.

"So, how's it going with you and Michelle?" I asked.

"None of your business. And you and Sally?"

"Nothing to report that's of any interest to you."

We also talked about the P.D.

I asked, "They reconsider hiring me back yet?"

Theo answered, "Excuse me, I didn't notice. When did hell freeze over?"

"So, is that a 'no'?"

His look was his answer, and the subject was dropped.

When we arrived at the Dragon, we stopped and gazed up at the massive steel beams and the twisting double-tube track. I shuddered, looking up at the place where my cart hung over the edge just a scant twenty-four hours before. Oh, I like the view you get from a great height, but I prefer a firm foundation under me. The hymn ran through my mind.

We searched the landscaped areas under the Dragon, trying vainly not to trample the foliage, but found nothing and left disappointed. Mr. Ozawa monitored our departure from in front of his potting shack, his eyes hidden by the shadow of his cap. He did not return my wave, but with his rake and pruning shears clutched tightly, set out to correct the damage we had done.

Theo said good-bye, told me it was a good theory and he was sorry it didn't pan out, then told me to keep in touch and to call him when I had another wild idea. I waved him off and returned to my office in Michelle's old trailer. I had barely made myself at home when the phone rang. It was Sally.

"Harry wants to see you."

"What about?"

"A special assignment." She didn't sound too excited.

"Okay," I sighed. "Be right over."

I cradled the receiver. Now what?

Eight

"Are you sure you want me to go?" I shifted uncomfortably in the chair opposite Harry's desk as he gazed at me with raised eyebrows.

"Yes," he answered. "Don't you want to go?"

"I . . . uh . . . well, it just seems like a job for someone — I don't know — higher up in the management structure."

"Don't worry about that," Harry assured, leaning back in his chair and interlocking his fingers across his plaid-shirted belly below the end of a too-short striped tie. He smiled at me in that way of his, that squint-eyed Snidely-Whiplash-and-the-Grinch-rolled-into-one grin, where the corners of his mouth curled slowly toward his ears, stretching his fat lips like a small ball of clay rolled between your hands into a snake. His upper lip finally disappeared altogether. I had the feeling he was throwing me to the wolves — and enjoying it.

"This isn't a public relations trip," he informed me. "I need you to finalize the security arrangements, get their itinerary down pat, go over the final details with them so we can make sure Mr. Hiromoto's visit here is safe and productive."

Without changing position, he reached out for a folder on his blotter and pushed it toward me.

"Everything you'll need is in there, including directions."

"What about a car?" I asked. "I really don't think my van would paint a positive picture of the park, you know what I mean? And it wouldn't fit in the underground parking downtown. Besides, I'd hate for it to break down on the way and make me late, or miss it altogether. I understand punctuality is a very big deal with the Japanese."

The smile faded from his lumpy face. "What about the BMW?"

"That's not mine, Harry, remember? I borrowed it from Trish and she's not in a position right now to loan it. Besides, I've imposed on her enough."

"Well, Sally will loan you her car. After all, you two are —"

"Are what?"

"You know. . . ." He winked.

"Well, Harry," I said slowly through clenched teeth, forcing myself to stay in the chair and keep my voice unemotional and at a low volume. It wasn't for myself that I took offense; he was impugning Sally's virtue. "With all due respect, in the first place, our relationship is none of your business. You know full well Sally doesn't tell me any management secrets. You would have transferred her long ago if you thought that. In the second place, you're just plain wrong. We're good friends and I have great respect for her and keep my hands to myself. And you can wink until your eye falls out. Our relationship is proper, and I resent your insinuation that it's otherwise."

"Whoa, settle down, Gil," Harry stammered, holding his hands up to fend off my ire. "I wouldn't care if you were —"

"Hogwash, Harry! If it didn't matter, you wouldn't have mentioned it."

"I was just saying, if you two were close — and I saw you kissing on the midway after the crash — then maybe you could use her car."

"Good grief, Harry. I don't have to take Sally for granted, you're doing it for me. There on the midway, we were both relieved I was safe. I'd've kissed you if you'd been the first one to greet me. Well, maybe not. But I've kissed lots of people that I wouldn't ask to borrow their car. And I've borrowed cars from people I would never kiss. Those two activities aren't related. But that's still not why I'm not going to borrow her car. Yeah, she'd let me. No problem. The point is, this is park business you're sending me on. If you want me to go — and I'll be happy to — then give me a car to get there. Good grief, Harry. Give me yours. You can do without it for one day."

He adjusted himself in his desk chair and cleared his throat. "Oh, well, of course. You're right. I'm sure we have a security vehicle we can spare."

If there's one thing I've learned over the years, it's that you can't separate a person of rank from their perks. When Harry went on vacation, he locked his company-owned sedan in his garage so no one would be tempted to actually put it to good use.

"Okay, that's fine," I concluded, reaching over to take the folder. "When is this gig?" I opened it to glance at the secrets within.

"Tomorrow, 10 A.M.," Harry said. "At the big, tall building that used to be part of America. Oh, and whatever you do, don't mention Pearl Harbor."

Did I detect a little cynicism in Harry's comment? I didn't respond to it, although I understood how he felt. His father was killed at Pearl Harbor. We're probably the only country in the world that sells its land and buildings to noncitizens — and we do so with wild abandon. I just don't think anyone should own us, any more than we should own them.

But, unlike my boss, I kept my mouth shut . . . for once.

Picking up the folder and excusing myself, I closed his door behind me as I nodded my way out. Sally, from her position in her cubicle behind her neat but paper-saturated desk, glanced up as I passed and smiled. I stopped — unable to cruise by without talking to her.

"How's Trish?" I asked.

"Better," Sally said with a sigh. "She was really shook up."

"I don't blame her. I was pretty scared myself."

"She's so young. I don't think she's ever had to face her own mortality before; not like that, at least. She's had a lot thrown at her this year. Everett's murder, her new responsibilities here at the park, her parents' leaving the country . . . wave after wave of change until nothing is the same, and then she had to deal with what she figured were improper feelings for you."

"Huh?"

"You didn't know?" Sally said matter-of-factly.

"She said something while we were hang-

157

ing up there, but I didn't pay much attention to it."

"Trish had a bout of infatuation over you. Probably more like a replacement father figure, but I doubt she realized that. You never noticed her behavior?"

"No," I said, a little emphatically but meaning it. "I didn't encourage it." I paused, then added, "At least, not consciously."

"Of course not," Sally said with a grin. When I began to stammer a protest, she laughed. I would have joined her, but I was feeling guilty, just in case I had inadvertently done something to send Trish a false signal. It wouldn't do to have the most important woman in my life thinking I was flirting with nineteen-year-old blondes.

"How did you know?" I asked. "I mean, why —"

"I could see it," Sally said. "But when you and I got closer, she realized there was no future in it and backed off. Physically, at least. Then we had a chat, and she apologized. That was a week or so ago."

"Whew," I breathed. "At least she didn't shoot you in the head like that gal in New York, Amy what's-her-name."

"You're a real comfort."

"I had no idea," I confessed. "Some detective. And I doubt I would've believed it if she'd told me. Let's face it, I look at myself in the mirror every morning."

"Scary thought," Sally said with a grin.

"Hey, it's not all that bad. Well, okay, maybe it is."

"You're good at detecting facts," Sally said. "But when it comes to women and their emotions, you're pretty much a rookie."

"Maybe if you guys were consistent, us men wouldn't have so much trouble. Look, thanks for telling me. I'm sorry. I'll be careful."

"Well, it's not going to matter. Trish is probably going to England after all."

"I thought she might. When?"

"As soon as she settles down a little, gets her nerves back in order. She's already phoned her mom and dad."

"Hmmm." Mixed emotions. I was happy for Trish. I thought she really wanted to go with her parents in the first place but stayed out of some sense of loyalty to me, and to the park, and perhaps even to the Currans. And very likely out of some need to maintain some sort of connection with Everett, with his memory. But that was proving difficult and essentially nonproductive. She was too close to his parents, his possessions, to his shrine on the Currans' piano, and it was torment. I didn't think it'd be long before she went to England anyway. The Dragon incident just gave her a shove.

And while happy for her, I was a little sad for myself. I'd miss her. We'd had an unusual relationship. But if what Sally said was true — and I had no reason to believe it wasn't — this was likely the best course for Trish.

"I think she's doing the right thing," I said. "Maybe she can get a fresh start."

"I'm green," Sally admitted coyly. "I've always wanted to go to Great Britain."

"And I've always wanted a BMW. Some people have it all, don't they? Well, we can commiserate with each other."

"Maybe one of these days we can take one of your famous road trips, fly to Germany and buy a BMW, then drive it to England."

"One of these days," I said, "when God gives me a gold mine. Until then, maybe I'll take you to Bodie. I could afford that."

"What's that?"

"A real ghost town in the eastern Sierra Nevadas. Totally desolate and eerie, not a tree in sight, twelve feet of snow in the winter."

"I'll pass," she laughed.

"And those are its good points," I added, getting up. "Well, gotta go. Duty calls."

"Have fun tomorrow."

"Thanks." I winked. "See ya, Sal."

As I turned to leave, I caught a glimpse out of the corner of my eye of something on top of Sally's metal file cabinet. It hadn't been there that morning. The object was a plastic device with an antenna and was flaked with soil. It sat on a piece of paper.

"Drop your radio in the mud?" I asked, nodding toward it. "You want me to clean it up for you?"

She followed my nod with her head. "Oh, that's not mine. It's going to Lost and Found. And I don't think it's a radio, at least not like any I've ever seen."

I leaned toward the black article, seeing two chrome levers sticking up out of the face. A radio control device, like they use for model airplanes.

"Lost and found?" I said. "Why would someone lose this in the park? What I mean is, why would someone bring a radio controller to the park in the first place? Where'd you get this?"

"Dave Whelan brought it in."

"Where'd he get it?"

Sally shrugged. "I don't know."

I plucked it off the file cabinet by the tip of the antenna. "I'll take care of it. See you later."

"Okay." Sally smiled. I'm sure she wondered why I wanted it, but she didn't ask.

Man, what a woman.

I stuck the controller in a plastic bag from an empty trash can and headed for Whelan's office. His secretary, Lois Schilling, was holding court behind her desk, looking very defensive and troubled as her head jerked up when I stepped through the door. For a split second she had that panicked look, like a deer frozen in headlights, then she recognized me and her whole upper body visibly relaxed. Another tense time for Dave Whelan and company, apparently.

She forced a smile. "Good morning, Mr. Beckman."

"Good morning." I smiled back. "And please, call me Gil. I'm just a worker bee. Is Dave in?"

"Yes, I think so. I mean, yes, he is." She laughed nervously. "I meant to say, I think he's free."

Dave was being careful about his visitors. This Dragon thing must be worrying him. Maybe his job was on the line. Shouldn't have been. It wasn't his fault someone wanted to mess with the ride. Of course, he could be considered responsible for letting people on it, and it wasn't outside the realm of possibility someone would sue, someone with overactive greedy glands. And around here, any time something goes wrong, some-one has to take the blame, and it usually isn't the person upon whose shoulders responsi-bility should alight.

So what's new?

Lois announced me and told me to go on in. Dave was definitely worried, judging by the look on his face, but appeared relieved to see me.

"Any news?" he asked as we shook hands.

"Not yet." I held the bag open and he peered in. "Where'd you find this?" I asked, getting right down to business.

"What is — oh, that thing. One of the sweepers dropped it off. Said he found it."

"Do you know where?"

"No, I don't. I mean, who cares? Why, is it important?"

"Don't know. But it's a remote controller for inexpensive R.C. planes or cars."

"R.C.?"

"Radio control. You know, model air-planes and stuff."

He looked at me quizzically, trying to un-derstand the significance.

"A remote control, one that could have been used to set off the charge," I explained.

The cloud of confusion fell from him, changing his expression to one of alarmed insight.

"You mean . . . ?"

"I don't mean anything. It's just a possibility. But why else would this be here? Let's face it, people don't come to the park to fly model airplanes or race their cars. Who was the sweeper who found this?"

"I-I don't know him."

"Did you see him, or did he drop it off with Lois?"

"Yes. No. What I mean is, he gave it to me, but I don't know his name. I think he's new. I don't recall seeing him before — no, wait a minute. His name tag said Joe, I think. Yeah, that's it. Joe. Oriental kid."

"Skinny?" I asked.

"Yeah."

"Okay, I think I know who that is. I saw him yesterday. I'll find him. Thanks a lot, Dave — oh, one more thing. The Dragon that crashed . . . had the carts been in the shop the day before?"

"Yes, as a matter of fact, they had. Is that important?"

"Don't know, Dave. Take care."

I left Dave to his troubles, nodding a friendly good-bye to the ever lovely Lois Schilling, and struck out through the screaming masses toward the sweeper shack.

The sweeper shack in the Boring 20s was

164

the main one. There were storage rooms all over, but this shack was home base for the sweepers. It was locked, but I had my security master keys — no one had ever asked for them back — and let myself in. The room was empty — devoid of humanity, that is. Rows of short brooms and those dustpans-on-a-stick lined the walls, next to bins of green plastic trash bags. Tacked on the wall, near the light switch, was a piece of paper. The schedule.

I ran my finger quickly down the names. Last name, first initial. Kang, J. and Saka-mura, Y. The rest of the names were Anglo or Hispanic.

The guy I had seen looked Japanese. Kang, now what was that, Korean or Chinese? I wasn't sure, but I knew it wasn't Japanese. And I doubted that Joe was his real name — his given name. He probably adopted that so Americans could pronounce it.

I called Sally on the park phone in the shack and had her run a quick check on both. Juni Kang and Yoshiyo Sakamura. Yoshiyo . . . Joe . . . an easy transition. I rechecked the schedule. He was on duty, assigned to the Wilderness Zone, the area the Dragon towered over, like the mythological winged beast that comes out of the mountain occasionally to terrorize the remote village it holds hostage, destroying houses with its flaming breath.

Strolling up the winding path through the Flapper Zone, I transitioned to a medieval European village while I chewed on a mustard-saturated corn dog and sucked grape drink from a green plastic jug shaped like a chubby Everett the dinosaur, and wished I was in shorts and a T-shirt like everyone else instead of a gray, double-breasted suit and silk tie with a red paisley pattern over a starched, white shirt. Boy, did I look out of place. I looked sharp, I admit. But out of place. Stuck out like a G-man at an outlaw biker bar. People who noticed me kept looking around for the President of the United States, I was so conspicuous.

When I got to the Wilderness, Yoshiyo Sakamura found me.

"You look for me?" he asked.

"Yeah, I was, actually," I said with suspicion. "How'd you know?"

"You look like detective, and I see that." He pointed to the semi-translucent plastic bag containing the radio controller. "You looking around like you are lost. I think maybe Mr. Whelan give it to you. You are police?"

"No, no, Mr. Sakamura —"

"Say, you know my name." He grinned.

166

"Call me Joe, okay?"

"Joe it is." I stuck out my hand and he pumped it vigorously. "I'm Gil Beckman. I work here. But I help the police sometimes. Like now. You're the one who found this?"

"Yes. Yes sir."

"Where?"

"Over here. Come, I show you."

He motioned for me to follow and trotted off toward the Dragon, waving his broom and dustpan behind him. His English was good but not great. It sounded like classroom English with little practical experience. Probably a foreign exchange student. We had quite a few of them working here because of the several colleges in the area. It was a status thing when they went back home. And it was a pretty good job, actually. Flexible hours, decent pay, good benefits, even for the part-timer.

The Dragon loomed over me as I followed Joe down into the landscaped area under the steel towers.

One of these days I'll ride that monster again, I told myself. If they ever open it, that is.

Joe was twenty or so, pale-skinned with short-cropped, dark hair. His slender body — five-foot-six or so — was covered by the dark blue trousers and short-sleeved, light blue shirt of the sweeper uniform, under which he wore a long-sleeved white T-shirt, even on a sunny day such as this. I couldn't blame him, though. With that pale skin, he'd burn easily, having to spend his whole shift out in the sun. Or it could be he'd started early in the day, when the coastal fog still chilled the air.

He stopped by a beautifully landscaped area at the far end of the ride, an area Theo and I had checked, and pointed to the middle of it.

"There," he said; then, anticipating my question, added, "I saw papers, went to pick up. There, in dirt." He pushed back some flowers with his broom. There was nothing unusual to be seen.

I glanced toward the loading dock — at least, in the direction of the loading dock. I couldn't see it from here. That fit my theory that the suspect didn't know we were on the ride.

Behind me there was a small shack, the landscapers' workroom. Next to it was another small building that looked just like it, except the door was double-padlocked. *What's in there?* — I started to ask myself, then it clicked.

It was the storage room for the weekly fireworks display.

"When did you find this?" I asked Joe,

holding up the bag.

"Yesterday morning, before park open." Okay, that explained why Theo and I didn't find it. It had already been removed, and the crime scene guys might not have looked this far away from the accident scene.

"Thanks, Joe," I said, and he bowed slightly and trotted back to the midway to resume working. When he looked back over his shoulder once, I was still watching him, and he waved.

I had to wait until he was out of sight. No sense arousing his curiosity about the un-marked fireworks shack.

I walked around the outside, checking the locks, which were secure, and noted that the landscape shed actually had a common wall with the explosives shack. Perhaps at one time it had even been one room. Fine bit of planning, that.

Not having a key for the proprietary fire-works shack but having one for the landscape shed — it took a maintenance key, the same key as the sweeper shack, and also operated janitorial storage rooms — I took the path of least resistance.

What I was looking for wasn't hard to find. Behind a potting bench, which I had to shove to the side — noting the telltale skidmarks which told me it had been moved before —

was a rectangular hole cut in the wall, then re-covered with the piece that had been cut out. The saw cut was irregular, done in a hurry. I removed the piece and saw that the hole had been cut between studs, yielding a fifteen-by-fifteen inch square to crawl through.

I fought the urge to do so. After all, I knew where it went. Plus, I was wearing my second-best suit.

It was time to call Theo in. Though still without a clue as to motive, we now, at least, had someone to question. I pulled the potting bench back in front of the makeshift hatch and turned to leave, just as a shaft of light from the opening door spread out across my body. Then a shadow darkened the doorway again.

"Yes?" the shadow said expectantly, but said no more. It was obviously my turn. I waited for a second for my eyes to adjust, then focused on the troubled face of Mr. Ozawa. *Well, of course,* I berated myself. *Who else would it be?*

"You remember me, don't you, Mr. Ozawa? Gil Beckman, park security?"

"Yes, of course." He came all the way in, still puzzled. "Why are you in here, Mr. Beckman? Did I leave the door unlocked?" He looked at the potting bench, then back at me. It was only a brief, fluttering movement of his eyes but was unmistakable. "Is everything okay?"

"Everything is fine. I'm doing some checking, is all. Are, uh, you going to be doing anything special for Mr. Hiromoto's arrival Saturday?"

"Special? Like what?"

"Oh, I don't know. Like any Bonsai displays or anything."

"No, we hadn't planned on any Bonsai. I'm sure Mr. Hiromoto gets enough of that in Japan."

"Of course," I agreed. "We want him to like the park the way it is, don't we?" I was sounding like an idiot, playing the role of the stupid American and doing it very well. I'd been around Jerry Opperman too much.

Ozawa was finished talking. Although he no doubt wasn't satisfied with my explanation for being in his shed, he did not question it further. I was, after all, his superior in the management structure of the park — in his mind, at least — and the Japanese are not typically given to questioning authority.

"Please," Ozawa said, gesturing politely to the door. "I have work. . . ." He trailed off but I got the point and dismissed myself without further comment.

I felt Ozawa knew why I was there, and he

knew that I knew about the crawl space to the fireworks, but I didn't want to tip my hand, not yet at least. Just outside the shed, though, I stopped and hailed Ozawa before he could close the door. I opened the plastic bag so he could look in.

"Have you seen this before?"

He glanced at the radio controller with no change of expression.

"No, Mr. Beckman, I haven't."

I expected him to ask why I wondered, but he said nothing, just looked at me blankly. I couldn't read into that. He may have just been trying to act nonplussed, but he may also have been telling the truth. I couldn't tell. That he didn't wonder why I'd asked him about the controller could have meant he already knew, or it could also mean he just didn't care. I could draw no conclusions.

I thanked him and headed for personnel. Once again, there was a file I needed to peruse.

Nine

The lobby floor of the skyscraper was covered with charcoal-colored marble streaked with white, the walls were a pale yellow, textured vinyl covering. Indirect lighting predominated and potted plants and trees were scattered throughout the room. A small carpeted area near a receptionist contained a few uncomfortable-looking chairs and glass-topped tables with boring magazines scattered across them. In the entire lobby, there was no hint of anything oriental, despite the Hiro Industries name on the outside of the building. Actually it just said HIRO, in hundred-foot, stylized, illuminated red letters at the top of the building and on a tasteful brass plate near the all-glass front entry.

I checked in with the security officer at the semicircular desk, avoiding the sultry receptionist who was admiring her reflection in the tinted windows, and who would probably just ask me to have a seat and wait. The armed, uniformed guard told me the person I wanted was on the top floor. *Naturally*, I thought, but I said thanks. To the right, he added.

Exiting the elevator after a lengthy ride — trying not to think about the vast abyss under my feet, from which I was separated by just an inch-thick plate of wood and steel — I stepped out onto more marble. There was a small NO SMOKING sign on the opposite wall in English and Japanese (I presumed it was Japanese), and to the left and right were sets of double doors. Tall, darkly stained, solid wood, ornate, with subtle filigreed designs that upon closer inspection looked to be oriental characters arranged vertically. Both sets of doors were otherwise unmarked.

Following the security officer's instructions, I passed through the set on the right.

A pretty, dark-haired receptionist greeted me. Her features were classic Japanese only very slightly so, and her hair was not quite black. I guessed her bloodline was somewhat mingled, and her soft voice bore no trace of an accent. By virtue of her apparent mixed heritage she had that mysterious, alluring, exotic look about her, and she seemed self-conscious about it. But she was very polite and took my name, then made a quiet call to someone and asked if I would have a seat. She offered me coffee, which I accepted, and she disappeared. When she returned in a few minutes, she carried a silver tray containing a small silver carafe and a dainty china cup with matching saucer. She poured the brew for me and handed it to me with a smile and a plate of genuine, imported English shortbread cookies, then returned to her station. I never got her name.

As I sat in the simple yet plush waiting area outside the office suite of the heir to the Hiromoto fortune, the door opened and a young Oriental man — again, presumably Japanese — motioned for me to follow. I set down the cup, snatched up one last cookie which I ate on the move, and followed him down a long corridor. I glanced through an open door as I passed and saw several men inside talking and drinking from small cups with no handles but didn't get a close look at them except to notice they wore slightly oversize black suits, just as my guide had on. One of the men had his back to me. His coat was off and his shirt sleeves were rolled up revealing slender but heavily tattooed forearms. He started to look at me but turned his head away quickly before I could catch his eye. I wondered about it but couldn't stop. Probably just some Eastern sign of respect: *not polite to stare at guest.*

Not that it's okay for Westerners to stare at guests, but, in general, Americans have no manners. We lost them when we threw aside our sense of modesty in the sixties and the women took off their bras. It was inevitable that a loss of social propriety would follow. Not so with people of other countries, particularly Asians. They still understand the importance of manners.

Americans of Japanese ancestry, who grew up here, aren't necessarily that way, unless they were raised by traditional parents. I hadn't known too many Japanese growing up. Not Japan Japanese, at least. There were always Japanese kids in school, but they were just as American as myself. Wore the same clothes, read the same books, watched the same movies . . . even talked the same. And I never met one who knew more than a word or two of Japanese. They were Americans, just as second- or third- or fourth-generation Italians or Jews or Czechs were Americans. It's just that the Japanese and other Asians couldn't blend in as easily because of their facial characteristics, and they were still looked upon by many as foreigners — and were expected to act as such. Whatever that meant.

We had arrived. The door opened and my guide stood back and allowed me to pass through. I smiled my thanks but it was not returned. He didn't glare or frown, he just maintained that expressionless visage. The door closed behind me and he was gone.

The office was a testimonial to Yuppie accessory catalogues, full of those totally nonessential yet really neat and expensive trinkets that validate their owner's position and power. It was a relatively dark place, with light coming from many of those trinkets, including the most awesome fish tank I'd ever seen outside of a public aquarium. To say it was filled with tropical fish would be an understatement. These were prehistoric-looking fish, fish in glorious Technicolor, fish dressed up for a Hollywood premier.

On an immense cherry desk sat a green and brass banker's lamp. It was on, and the light illuminated the face of my host, Eric Hiromoto, grandson and heir to the fortune of Kumi Hiromoto, founder of the empire.

He was resplendent in his gray, double-breasted Armani suit. I supposed it was an Armani. Guys like this would wear nothing else. For all I could tell by looking at it, he got it at a thrift store. But it looked good to me all the same.

"Welcome, Mr. Beckman," Mr. Hiromoto said, rising and extending a hand across the desk. A gold chain encircled his wrist.

"Good morning, sir," I returned. "Pleasure to meet you."

"I was just about to order lunch. Would you care to join me?"

I had visions of a platter of raw fish. "Uh, no thank you, Mr. Hiromoto," I said, glancing at the aquarium.

He followed my gaze and smiled. "I take it you don't like *sashimi*."

"You mean *sushi*, don't you?"

"A common misconception, I'm afraid. *Sashimi* is uncooked fish. *Sushi* is the little rice and seaweed rolls and other such delicacies that are often stuffed with *sashimi*."

"Oh. Well, I never tried either one," I admitted. "If they would take the *sashimi* and batter dip it and pop it in the deep fryer, then serve it in a plastic basket on a bed of french fries, I might be tempted."

Hiromoto laughed. "Actually, I was going to have a submarine sandwich."

"No thanks, just the same," I said. I hated eating in front of important people. My chin wrinkled when I chewed, and I looked stupid.

"Very well. Shall we proceed, then? Please, sit down."

The burgundy, leather, wingback chair took me in and caressed me as I sat, creaking ever so elegantly. I wondered that Eric Hiromoto had lost all traces of any accent, then remembered from his bio that he had not only been educated here but had been raised here from the age of ten.

"I've got to tell you, sir, you're not at all what I expected," I admitted, feeling comfortable with him.

"You were expecting, maybe, Charlie Chan's number one son?"

"I doubt it," I said, raising my guard a little. "He's Chinese, is he not?"

Eric Hiromoto smiled slyly. "Yes, that is true. But we are all the same to white people, for the most part. At least, that is what they say."

I had the feeling he was testing me, or trying to put me on the defensive, just so he could feel like he was in control. Up until now things had been cordial. But he was beginning to jockey for position, probably a habit that conducting high-dollar business had developed in him. Frankly, I didn't care who was in control. This was his castle, and he was the king. But I had a job to do here, and I wasn't in the mood for games.

"That's a fairly narrow-minded statement, sir," I said quietly. "I don't appreciate the assumption that, because I'm white, I don't like the Japanese, or think I'm smarter than the Japanese, or can't tell the Japanese from the Chinese or Korean. I'm not here because you're Japanese. Frankly, I couldn't care less.

If you were a talking giraffe it wouldn't make any difference to me. I'm here because you and your grandfather are to be very important guests of the park, and your safety is a major concern to us. So if you can dispense with the posturing and the mind games, let's get down to business. That okey-dokey with you?"

Eric Hiromoto considered me blankly, then his mouth slowly managed a slight smile. "Okey-dokey," he parroted. "I like you, Mr. Beckman. You speak your mind. That's rare in my circles."

"I'm sorry to hear that."

"Me too. But in the world of business, especially Japanese business, to speak one's mind can give your opponent an advantage."

I wasn't going to suggest that the alternative was to lie, because I didn't think he meant that. To simply tell another what they wanted to hear, especially if it would be advantageous to do so, was not considered lying by the Japanese, especially if most or part of what you said was true.

It's just that the Japanese — by virtue of our lack of understanding of their culture, which makes them seem "inscrutable" and "mysterious" — seem to have a knack for the practice of telling only as much truth as they think you have a right to hear. That's just the way they do business, and we need to understand these things to get along.

Eric Hiromoto, however, was raised and educated here. I suspected that he was as Americanized as myself.

Basically, my initial appreciation for the younger Hiromoto quickly became dislike, but since my feelings for him had nothing to do with my duties here, I shrugged them off. His approach to business, or to life, wasn't my problem.

Hiromoto then said, "Would you like something to drink?" as if the conversation we'd just had never took place.

"Some tea, please, if you have any."

"I believe we can scrape some up," he said wryly. "But I'm afraid it's all British in origin. Imported Earl Grey."

"That'll be fine," I consented. "And I wouldn't mind a couple of those little cookies —"

"Fortune cookies are traditionally Chinese."

"I meant those shortbread things."

"Of course," he said demurely. A valet appeared, Hiromoto whispered a few instructions, and the valet was gone. Mr. Hiromoto smiled at me across the desk. "Down to business, then. What have you planned for us, Mr. Beckman?"

I opened the folder and spread it out for him: the day's itinerary, which rides to visit and when, shows to see, food to eat. It had all been painstakingly plotted to provide maximum effect, to let him see and hear and taste and feel the best of the park, while avoiding those things he might not appreciate. Roughly translated, the junky attractions.

The valet returned and left the tray on the edge of the desk. We helped ourselves in silence.

"Very impressive, Mr. Beckman," Hiromoto said presently, leaning back and absentmindedly stroking his fifty-dollar power tie. "But we had in mind something less structured. For example, I imagine Grandfather and I would like to eat when we are hungry, not when it is convenient for our hosts." He leaned forward. "I notice also that some of your rides are not listed. For example, the Dinosaurs, where are they? Don't be concerned about the Japanese and their love of Godzilla. We would not be offended. In fact, my grandfather told me to be sure he meets this Everett of yours. That's part of the reason for his interest in the park. And when Grandfather saw the picture in the paper, of Everett capturing the robber, he was delighted."

I groaned inwardly, then thought, *Oh well, at least it won't be me in that suit.* I wondered, *Did the old man actually think Everett was real or something?* Surely not.

Eric Hiromoto continued. "And the Dragon. What about it?"

"We didn't think your, uh, Mr. Hiromoto would be interested in riding a roller coaster."

"His age is your concern?"

"Well, yes."

"Don't underestimate my grandfather. He's as strong as he was half a lifetime ago. You see, Mr. Beckman, he doesn't want to build a park like yours in Japan just to make money. He wants to *go there,* to have fun, to enjoy life."

"Interesting," I said. "Well, I certainly don't care what you want to do. It's up to you. But you need to understand that having you there is a liability of sorts — it's always a liability to have famous, influential, or otherwise important people visit the park — and as such, we must maintain a modicum of control over your movements. At the very least, several of us will accompany you, closely. And there will be some sort of schedule, however flexible you wish to make it. Those two factors cannot be eliminated, I'm sure you understand that."

I took a sip of tea but held his gaze. He waited patiently for me to continue, for me to make my case. I almost wished he was a suspected killer and I was given the task of interrogating him. He believed himself to be important and powerful — and above me in all qualities — and those kind of people are a challenge, because they really want to discuss their crime, to gloat about it, but they want to make the cop earn the right to ask them questions. And they especially love to pull the wool over their interrogator's eyes. What makes them so much fun is that they are so full of themselves that they become overconfident and are hardly ever adept enough to outsmart a good interrogator. Look at television's Columbo, a great example of the kind of cop I'm talking about, even if he is a caricature, exaggerated for the sake of entertainment.

But Eric Hiromoto was not a suspect, and I would have to be satisfied with this little exchange.

"I noticed upon arriving," I continued, "that the way into your office was not open to me. I was required to go through several reception areas, and then was not permitted to walk freely about. I was led in by one of your . . . assistants. I presume that is all to preserve your safety, as well as your privacy?

You have recognized certain liabilities that accompany money and power, in addition to certain luxuries, and have responded accordingly by reducing the risks."

Hiromoto grinned and drummed his fingers together in front of his chest.

"Your point is well taken," he said. "I will do as you ask. If you will leave these items, I will bring a revised — but not ironclad — schedule with me when we arrive Saturday. We will be there at ten o'clock. I trust you will meet us?"

We both stood, and Hiromoto reached across the desk to shake my hand. I took it firmly, but not overly so, allowing Hiromoto to set the standard for grasping firmness and keeping my grip just less than his. I noted in my peripheral vision the hint of a tattoo on his wrist, peeking out beyond the French cuffs of his silk shirt, but did not see it well enough to guess what it might be.

"I'll be there," I said.

Back at the park I reported in to Harry, telling him that Eric Hiromoto would be going over the plan and making a few changes. I didn't tell him how extensive they would be, because I really didn't know. I did say that he wanted to be inconspicuous and let Harry figure out for himself what that meant.

It had been a long day, even though my audience with Hiromoto Double-Junior had only lasted a couple hours. I'd had to fight the traffic both ways, and that, added to my two adventures from the days past, had driven my stress level up a notch or two.

I was tired, and I wanted to rest a little before Sally and I went to the Currans' for a barbecue. I asked Harry if I could split early, and he said okay.

I wanted to get out of there fast before he came to his senses. Unfortunately, there was a phone call for me. It was Theo.

Ten

Lt. Theo Brown sounded tired over the phone. I didn't know what else he had going but couldn't imagine this case occupying much of his time.

"We got a print off the controller," he told me. "Where'd you touch it?"

"The tip of the antenna," I said. "But Sally, Rides Chief Dave Whelan, and the kid that found it, Joe Sakamura . . . they all handled it."

"It's not yours. It was on the body of the unit. We'll have to get their prints for elimination. I'll have my secretary make the appointments."

"So what do you think?"

"About what?"

"My theory."

"I think that's all it is."

"You got a better one, Kojak?"

"No, not yet. I have to admit, it's not so far-fetched that I can disregard it completely."

"Thank you for that, professor," I said with the slightest hint of sarcasm. "Look, he's got access to explosives, the device was hidden in an area only he frequents, he was present at the time —"

"And nothing else. A lot of people have a key to the landscape shack, you told me so yourself. We found no prints in the fireworks shack, although I do believe it may not have been a blasting cap after all. There was absolutely no evidence of a blasting cap in the wreckage. It's possible the perp could've used fireworks powder, packed a little of it into something like a pipe bomb. The pieces of that could have been launched and not fallen straight down. Someone might not recognize them for what they are and just throw them away. For now, I'll go with that as the most likely possibility, especially in light of that crawl space. But Ozawa is certainly not the only one who had access, since all the maintenance guys and sweepers and custodians carry the same key, not to mention the security officers with their masters — such as yourself."

"Don't start," I warned. "I've been suspected enough times without this. Remember, I was on the Dragon when it blew."

"I was joking." He coughed, and during a pause I heard a cigarette lighter flick.

"What about footprints in the fireworks shack?"

"Yeah, there were scuffs," Theo said. "Someone definitely used the hatch to get in. So what? That was a given as point of entry. But we don't know they got in to steal fireworks to blow up the Dragon. Employee theft is a problem. Someone might be selling the fireworks to another amusement park. Besides, there were no discernable prints clear enough for comparison. What we're going to need is a motive after all, I'm afraid. I checked Ozawa's record. He's clean as a whistle."

"I looked up his application," I told Theo. "Did you know he has a master's degree in electrical engineering from USC? He also used to work in the aerospace industry. Left it five years ago."

"So what's he doing working as a land-scaper?"

"That's the $64,000 question, Theo. And I think I know who to ask."

"Who?"

"Better you don't know. I'll call you when I find out something." I hung up before he could yell at me.

Michelle Yokoyama looked up from a piece of steno paper covered with notes and figures, drawing me into the room with her smile.

"Gil, please, come on in."

"Excuse me, I didn't mean to disturb you."

"Nonsense. This stuff is giving me a headache. I'm glad to have an excuse to put it aside for awhile." She straightened the papers and pushed them away from her, turning the top sheet over so she wouldn't be tempted to peek at it. Or so I wouldn't.

"Did Harry get with you?" she asked.

"Not yet. At least not about my assignment."

"I'm sure he will soon, as soon as this . . . business is behind us." She waved her hand daintily, and I took her to mean Saturday's visit by Hiromoto. I nodded, and she said, "What's on your mind, Gil?"

"Well, to tell the truth, I need to ask you about someone you know who works here."

"Oh? Who?"

"George Ozawa, the landscaper."

"George? He's like an uncle to me. Why do you need to ask about him?"

"You got him his job here, is that correct?"

"I recommended him, yes. He got the job on his own merits." Her posture stiffened and her tone of voice suddenly had an edge to it. She didn't waste any time nailing me down.

"Gil, you're not asking about him out of social interest. That's not your style. What's going on?"

I knew I wouldn't get any more from her without telling her everything. Well, most everything. There's just no way of telling how much might get back to him. I took a deep breath.

"Michelle, Theo and I have come up with some evidence that might implicate Mr. Ozawa in some way in the sabotage of the Dragon. I know, I was shocked too and don't want to believe it. The problem we have is that we can't ignore it. We have to check it out."

"Why not ask George?"

"I don't want to upset him unnecessarily. If he's innocent, it's better he not know about our inquiry, so he doesn't worry."

"Did Theo ask you to question me?"

"No, he didn't. And he doesn't know I'm here. I just thought it'd be better for me to do it. I wouldn't want there to be a . . . problem between you two, if you know what I mean."

She relaxed a little but didn't drop her guard. "Yes, I can see that, but —"

"It's just as important, Michelle, to clear Mr. Ozawa. Any investigation is a search for truth, not just an attempt to nail someone."

"Okay, Gil, I trust you in that. But . . . George Ozawa? I mean, he couldn't hurt anyone. He's probably the kindest man I ever met."

"No doubt, Michelle."

I didn't see the point in telling her that there were people who said the same thing about virtually every killer ever caught. I guarantee, if the victims could talk, they'd paint an entirely different picture. Since they can't, the police do it for them. And without absolute proof to Ozawa's guilt, I didn't want to give her second thoughts about him.

I said, "That's why I need to ask you about him, so we can eliminate him."

"Okay," she said with a sigh. "What do you need to know?"

"Just some background, really. How long have you known Mr. Ozawa?"

"All my life. He's older, but we are essentially of the same generation, and played together as kids. He even babysat me. Our mothers were best friends, had been since they were children."

"So, he was born in . . . ?"

"December, 1942."

The question that knowledge prompted would be a tough one — tough to ask and tough to answer — so I put it off.

"He went to USC. Has an engineering degree."

"Yes."

I studied her face, finally raising my eyebrows and asking the obvious. "So what's he doing here?"

"I never asked him, Gil. But I can tell you he is happy."

"Has he a wife? Kids?"

"A grown son, back East. His wife died in a car wreck five years ago."

I looked at his park records. "About the same time he came here," I stated matter-of-factly.

"Sounds like someone else I know," Michelle commented without malice.

"Just an observation," I said. "Not a cause for suspicion."

"He's always loved gardening," Michelle said. "Aerospace is a difficult industry to work in. He was laid off shortly before she died. In fact, she had to get a job and was on her way to work when she died. I know he blames himself for that. He never said so, but I think that all contributed to his coming here. He's always loved gardening, as I said, and with her gone, he didn't need the big house and couldn't afford it. When he moved to a small apartment, he could no longer garden. Put it all together and his coming here makes a lot of sense."

I nodded. She was right, it made sense. "Yes, seems pretty straightforward. To your knowledge, does he know Kumi Hiro-moto?"

"How could he? George has never left the country."

"Was his mother in Manzanar with your parents?"

I had slipped the question in without apology, keeping my eyes on my papers so she wouldn't feel the pressure of my gaze, a tactic I reserved for suspects. But there was no immediate response from her, so after a moment or two, I lifted my eyes casually. She was looking away.

"Yes," she said when she returned her eyes to mine. They had been focused on the window toward the atrium, where a new Japanese garden had been designed and installed by Mr. Ozawa.

"So he was born there," I concluded.

"Yes."

"You said your mother and his were best friends. What happened to his father?"

"Killed during the war. All I know is, he was with the all-Japanese regiment fighting in Italy. The 442nd. That's about all I can tell you, Gil. For the rest, you'll have to ask him."

"His mother never remarried?"

"No. Not that I'm aware of. She died shortly before his wife."

I closed my folder. "Okay, Michelle. That helps."

"What is the evidence?"

"Circumstantial at this point." I told her about the radio controller and the explosives shack. I also cautioned her. "Michelle, I'm going to have to ask you not to say anything to Mr. Ozawa. What I've told you is privileged information. I only told you because you're a friend, and I know Mr. Ozawa is a friend of yours. If he is innocent, I'll prove it. Okay?"

She hesitated. "Yes, I understand. But he absolutely is innocent. I'm positive of that."

For her sake, I hoped she was right.

I left the park to drive home for a quick shower. I still had an hour or two before Sally and I had to be at the Currans' house. On my way out, though, I saw Joey Duncan walking home. I pulled the van over to the curb and honked.

Joey looked around, saw it was me, and ambled over. Without comment, he climbed in.

"Want a ride?" I asked sarcastically.

"Yeah. How'd you know?"

"Lucky guess. Where to?"

"Home, I guess," he said, shrugging.

I had a sudden inspiration and drove off

without comment but did not make the turn that would have taken us to his house.

"You missed the turn, Mr. Beckman," he said laconically.

"Yeah. I know."

He glanced around, then said with suspicion, "So where are we going?"

"It's no big deal," I told him. "I just want to show you something, then I'll take you home, or wherever you want to go."

He grunted but didn't respond. A mile or two later I asked him how the cartooning was going. His attitude changed, mellowing out and brightening up.

"It's a lot of fun. Especially since I get to draw stuff for other things, too."

"Like what?"

"You know, the junk they sell here. T-shirts and plates and puzzles and stuff. I just sit there all day cranking it out. Everett doing this, Everett wearing that, Everett on the rides, Everett in his time machine, Everett in the wild West . . . you name it. Some of it they ask for, some of it I think of myself."

"Sounds good. How's the art class the park is sending you to?"

"That's real cool. I had no idea there were so many different things to use."

"Other than cans of spray paint, you mean?"

"Yeah." He grinned sheepishly. "You want to hear something funny? You know that warehouse wall you can see from the street? They want me to paint a mural there . . . using spray paint. Isn't that cool?"

"You're certainly qualified. And the nice thing is, you won't have to do it with one eye looking over your shoulder for the cops." We laughed, and I said, "I'm glad it's working out for you, and you're having a good time."

"Yeah, thanks. I . . . uh . . . I appreciate you getting me the job, man."

"You're welcome."

As we approached a freeway underpass I noticed a slight smile tickle the corners of his mouth, but he quickly put his hand up to wipe it away. Going under the freeway I saw a spray-painted mural on the wall: a highly detailed picture with shading and good perspective — of a cartoon dinosaur that looked all too familiar. I gave Joey a glare out of the corner of my eye but said nothing. He looked away absently, but I could tell he was fighting a grin.

When we arrived at our destination and parked the car, I said, "Up in smoke," and got out.

"What are you talking about?" he asked.

"Your career, if you can't kick the habit.

If you get caught, it's curtains."

"That's the last one, honest," Joey assured. "Check it out. It says 'good-bye' in the corner by my name."

"You put your name on it? You're dumber than I thought."

"Not my real name, my tagging name."

"Your moniker. And just what is your moniker?"

He grinned, as big as I've ever seen him grin. "Gilbert Beckman."

Something told me I'd be buying a can of spray paint on the way home.

"So what is this place?" Joey asked.

"It's a store for backpackers, hikers, campers, that kind of thing."

"What are we doing here?"

"You'll see."

We went inside the gigantic store. There were canoes, tents, sleeping bags, mountain bikes and clothing, books, backpacking supplies . . . everything for the outdoors. In the rear corner was a rock-like wall to the ceiling, about twenty feet high. It was man-made to simulate a vertical rock face, with hand- and toeholds bolted onto it that could be moved to provide new and different challenges. Above, spanning the two right-angle walls, was a block and tackle that could be attached to a harness worn by the climber to prevent a mishap should they slip, or fall off. The floor beneath was padded to lessen the shock of landing. A muscular attendant welcomed us. His name tag introduced him as Craig.

"Think you could climb it?" I asked.

"Easy," he said.

I nodded to the attendant, who handed the harness to Joey.

"I don't need that," Joey said.

"I'm sure," Craig said, still smiling. "Insurance requires it."

"Oh, all right." He stepped into it.

"It's different than what you're used to," I cautioned. "There are no girders to stand on or grab. It's all toes and fingertips."

Joey ignored me and started up the wall, got about three feet before he lost his footing and slipped off. He tried it again with the same result.

"Okay," he told Craig. "I'll let you do your job. What's the secret?"

"Go slow, keep your arms and feet spread as far as you can so your body lies flat. Upper body strength is very important. Wedge your feet into the cracks so you can push up — and go slow. Don't try moving until you're ready."

"Okay, that's enough."

He started up again, got halfway this time before running out of toeholds.

"You can't always go straight up," Craig said. "To your right, that crevice. Stick your foot in there. Yes, that's right. Good."

Joey made it. He was red-faced and sweating, but he made it.

"Jump off," the attendant said. "Just push away from the wall. You'll come down slow."

"I'll climb," Joey insisted.

"It's harder than going up."

The attendant was right. Joey missed his second foothold and down he came, kept from a hard landing by the harness and the attendant's hold on the rope.

"That was great for a first-timer!" Craig said, pumping Joey's hand. "Most folks can't make it all the way up without help."

"He's had lots of practice," I said, drawing a glare from Joey. I didn't expound, but gave the lad an exaggerated, closed-mouth grin.

"Can I try again?" Joey asked the attendant.

"Sure. Have at it. Why don't you try this line over here?" he suggested. "It's a little tougher."

"Okay. No problem."

It was, though. He didn't even get halfway until the third assault.

Later, as Joey removed the harness, a little dejected, I patted him on the shoulder. "Keep practicing, Joey. I might be going fishing sometime soon, and there's lots of places to climb where I'm going. You interested?"

"Just us?"

"Probably not. Mr. Curran will be going. His son runs the resort at the lake."

"Do I have to fish?"

"Not if you don't want to. I thought you might like to try it, at least, though."

"Yeah, I guess."

"Good. Why don't you see if there's any equipment you can pick up while you're here. Maybe some shoes or gloves."

"I'm kind of . . . saving my money."

"That's good. For anything in particular?"

"An apartment."

"Trouble at home?"

"Same old stuff. Dad's drinking is getting worse, and he and my stepmom go at it all the time. The other day he told me I was old enough to move out. So I thought I would."

"Probably a good idea," I agreed. "And he's right, you are old enough. You've got a full-time job, it's time you were responsible for yourself." I thought a second. "When's your birthday?"

"In a couple months."

I turned to Craig. "Get him a decent pair of shoes and gloves, within reason. It's on me."

"Hey," Joey protested, "you don't have to do that, man."

"I know. I want to. It's your early birthday present, no strings. By the time your birthday rolls around, I may not be able to afford it."

He regarded me for a moment, then said, "Man, I don't get you. One day you're threatening to throw me in the hole, the next day you're buying me stuff. What's the deal?"

"The deal is you, Joey. You are what's changing, not me. And I like the direction you're going."

He grunted, and tried to act tough, but there was no mistaking the softening of his eyes.

"Thanks, man," he said softly. As he turned to follow the attendant to the shoe display I would have sworn he wiped a tear out of his eye. I know I did.

Eleven

A couple hours later I returned to the park and picked Sally up in the behemoth. She offered her car, but I declined.

"I'm worried about you," she said gently. "You could get stranded in this van somewhere."

"It's given me a lot of miles," I testified in the Ford's defense.

"Yes, but all good things must end someday. At least as far as cars are concerned."

"I can't afford a new one," I explained. "Especially now."

She was quiet, and I figured she knew about my being sent back to security, and that it would undoubtedly mean a cut in pay. But I didn't press her for details. That wouldn't be right, asking her to violate the confidence that being Harry's secretary involved. And it would put a strain on her, wanting to tell me what she knew but unable to do so. So I didn't ask, and she dropped the subject, and we rode to the Currans' in quiet conversation about other things.

We were greeted at the door by Estelle

Curran, who ushered us in, delivering hugs to both of us and a kiss to Sal, then offered chairs and iced tea. I asked where Harold was.

"In the backyard, fussing with the barbecue."

"I'll help," I offered, and left the women to sort out the kitchen details.

Harold Curran wore his barbecue apron, which proclaimed him to be the "Grill Sergeant," and had his barbecue fork in one hand and a mitten on the other. On the large covered barbecue with one of those side-burner things and all the other stuff, five big, thick, juicy, deliciously nonvegetarian steaks sizzled and smoked. The drool ran down my chin and I prayed sorrowfully for those unfortunates who thought eating only things grown in dirt was somehow a better way.

"Hey, Gil! Glad to see you!" Harold shouted.

I believed he was. "The steaks look great, Hal. I can hardly wait to sink my chompers into one."

"They'll be done in a jiffy."

"Anything I can do to help?"

"Nope. It's under control. How do you like yours?"

"Just the other side of pink. When it stops mooing, it's done."

"I like mine to give milk." He laughed. "Estelle has to have it brown. Yuck. I hate ruining meat like that."

"Sally too. What is it with women? Don't they know that makes it harder to chew?"

"Maybe that's why," Mr. Curran suggested. "They need to keep their jaw muscles in shape so they can yak."

In a few minutes the steaks were done to perfection, and we all assembled around the dining room table. A pale, subdued Trish joined us, looking none the worse for the wear. She tried to be apologetic again about taking me to the brink of death, but I put my arm around her shoulder and gave her a squeeze and told her to forget it. God had protected us and no real harm was done. She smiled weakly and didn't say much more.

No sooner had we sat down than the doorbell rang. It was a young man in a cheap polyester suit, carrying a thick, well-worn Bible. Estelle greeted him like an old friend and invited him to supper.

"Oh, I can't," we heard him say, sounding for all the world like he was hoping to be convinced to give in.

"Nonsense," Estelle replied.

"Oh, well, I suppose it would be all right," the man said in a strong show of resistance. "It smells awfully good."

She led him into the dining room and introduced him to Sally and me as Roger Stevens, the new pastor of the Currans' church.

"I'll toss another steak on the grill," Harold Curran said. "Just take a minute."

"Let me," I volunteered. "You've done enough, it's my turn. The coals should be perfect by now."

"What coals?" Hal said. "Just turn the knobs and press the red button. It'll fire right up. Instant barbecue."

I cooked the steak and brought it in to the appreciative young pastor and rejoined the group. Besides the steaks, there were potatoes, onions, corn-on-the-cob, fresh baked bread, and, waiting in the wings for later when we sat around the living room and gossiped, hot apple pie with melted cheddar cheese and a large dollop of hand-cranked vanilla ice cream, to be washed down with flavored coffee. And after all that, we'd each vow to go on a diet the next day.

If that wasn't Christian fellowship, I didn't know what was.

Hal asked the pastor if he wouldn't mind saying grace. Naturally he didn't and offered a lengthy blessing on the food, the day, our health, every missionary on the planet by name, and all the ships at sea. When he finished, we reverted to our primal instincts and dug into the grub with wild abandon.

Except me. When everyone looked up after the *amen* my head was resting comfortably on my still empty plate, and I appeared to be fast asleep.

"Just ignore him, Pastor," Mrs. Curran said while reaching for the platter of steaks to pass around. "Gil's a little irreverent. Once you get to know him you'll understand."

Trish giggled, which was a sign that she might be coming around, and the pastor blushed.

"I guess it was a little long," he apologized.

I soon found out Stevens was a recent seminary graduate with one year of experience as a youth pastor when the Currans' church called him to be the pastor. He was young and enthusiastic with a pocketful of dreams, a heart full of good intentions, and a brain full of Bible verses. All he lacked was some life experience.

"I understand you used to be a police officer," he said to me midway through the meal.

"Yes sir."

"What exactly did you do?"

"Police work, mostly."

"Gil," Sally warned softly.

"All right, dear. I was a homicide detective, Pastor."

"Oh, my. Well . . . I, uh . . . it certainly must've been exciting."

I thought about the Currans and decided not to educate the pastor about the realities of the job, not just now.

"It has its moments." I took a bite of steak and changed the subject. "So tell me, Hal. How's the fishing up at your son's place this season?"

"He tells me you almost don't need bait, they're biting so good."

"Sounds great."

"Fishing is God's way of getting men to relax. There's no earthly purpose for fish other than getting caught by men like us. Speaking of which, you could use a vacation, Gil," Mr. Curran concluded.

"Yes," Sally agreed. "You've been working too hard."

"And had several frightening ordeals," Estelle Curran added, just in case I had forgotten.

"I have to admit, it sounds inviting," I admitted. I knew we'd be going sometime, as I'd told Joey. But not this soon. I said, "I've got a lot of work to do at —"

"Nonsense. Let's plan that fishing trip," Mr. Curran said. "How about next week?"

"That's just too soon," I said. "I've got something to do this weekend at the park, and I'll need a few days to get ready besides."

"Week after, then," he decided. "I'll call Randy, have him reserve a cabin for us. What about you, Pastor? Care to go?"

"Thanks, but it's a little early in my career at the church to be taking a vacation," Pastor Stevens explained. "Besides, I'm a fisher of men."

And I'll bet he tells whoppers about his catch, I thought involuntarily, true to my tendency to think the worst about people. But I kept it to myself, just in case the devil had put that thought into my head.

"That's fine, maybe next time," Hal said. "Gil, why don't you call that Joey kid, see if he wants to go."

"He doesn't like fishing," I warned.

"Only because he never tried it, I'll bet. What does he like to do?"

"I think he wants to get into rock climbing."

"Great! There's plenty of rocks up there. We'll do some fishing, some hiking, some rock climbing —"

"Not you, Harold Curran!" Estelle asserted.

He laughed. "Don't worry, sugar. I'll just watch. I'm too old to be trying to climb rocks. It's all I can do to get up the front steps. Gil here, he can go up with the kid. He's young and strong."

"I've had my share of treacherous heights, thank you," I said. "But I'll be happy to help you watch Joey. It might be good for him to get away. With his family being like it is, who knows when he's been on a real vacation. I'll talk to him. Truth is, I mentioned the possibility to him just last night."

"It's settled, then," Mr. Curran said. "Mom, I think it's time for your pie."

We retired to the living room while Estelle and Sally prepared the dessert. Trish only nibbled at hers. She was pale and appeared tired, probably due in part to the medication that had been prescribed to keep her calm. It wasn't long before she bowed out and retired to her room. Mrs. Curran went with her, returning moments later.

"She's asleep already, poor dear. She's doing better, though. Gil got her to laugh tonight, and that's what she needs. The accident really shook her up."

The Currans were especially concerned about Trish, Estelle more than her husband. Not that Sally and I weren't, but we were both confident she'd be fine. Harold and Estelle were concerned as parents would be. Since Trish's folks had moved to England

and Trish stayed behind, the Currans had given her a place to stay. They had wisely not given her the room formerly occupied by their murdered son Everett — with whom Trish had had a budding relationship — but fixed up their other son's former bedroom, the one who ran the fishing lodge at the lake.

But things were not going well, despite the Currans' best intentions and efforts.

"The memory is too strong here," Estelle told us as she settled into her rocker and we began seconds of pie and coffee. "We love her so and want her to stay, but she's a lady now, should be on her own. It just isn't working here."

"Everything remind her of Everett?" I surmised.

Mrs. Curran smiled a bittersweet smile and glanced over my shoulder at a bank of photos of Everett on top of the piano.

"She doesn't want to forget, of course," Mr. Curran said, "but sometimes it's best not to be assailed with it all the time. It's difficult for us, naturally, but in a way it's more difficult for her, because she never had a chance to really get to know him, and she feels cheated. We tried taking the photos down but it didn't seem to make a difference. In fact, Trish put them back up. And now, since the accident, well. . . ."

"She's a sensitive gal," Sally said. "She told me about the photo business the other day. I think she knows how much those pictures mean to you. You know, she really wants to be okay — for you to be okay, too. She loves you both."

"We know that," Estelle said. "And we love her."

"It's probably going to work itself out real soon," I interjected, now that I had finished my pie.

"How so?" Hal asked.

"When we were hanging in space, she expressed regret that she hadn't gone to England with her parents. Naturally, when you're caught in an avalanche, you wish you'd gone to the beach instead. But I think she'll still feel the same in a week or so when she's calmed down."

"Maybe it was a sign from God," ventured Pastor Stevens.

"Maybe," I said. "Whether it was or not, I think it's the right thing to do if she feels strongly enough about it."

"Why don't we pray for her?" Sally suggested. "Gil?"

"Certainly." I set down my plate — it was empty anyway — and we bowed our heads. "Lord and Father, we hold up Trish before you. Strengthen her, give her grace and peace to recover from the effects of the accident, to come out of it emotionally, mentally and spiritually intact, and to know what decision she should make about staying here or leaving for England to be with her parents. And help all of us Lord . . . the Currans especially . . . give them strength to deal not only with the loss of their son but with the loss of Trish as well should she decide to leave. Be with Sally as she counsels Trish. Give her wisdom and the ability to give wise counsel. Lord, thank You for the salvation You provided, and for Your mercy yesterday in keeping us all safe during our ordeal. Watch over Trish, and in all things, may Your will be done. In the name of our Lord and Savior Jesus Christ, Amen."

They chorused the *amen* and we all looked up. Estelle discreetly wiped a tear from her cheek. Sally took a deep breath. I glanced at my plate and coveted another hunk of pie but held my peace.

"So how does that barbecue work, Hal?" I asked, changing the subject. "That push-button thing I mean. That beats lighting a match and having the gas send a ball of flame up your sleeve, or fussing with charcoals. For me, it just isn't worth it to barbecue that way. I waste too much in briquets and lighter fluid."

"It's great!" Harold said. "We barbecue just about everything, don't we dear?" Estelle nodded. " 'Cept chili."

"You tried once," Estelle reminded him.

We laughed, and Harold blushed. "It's not what you think," he told us. "I had it wrapped in aluminum foil so it wouldn't slip through the grill. Anyway, Gil, to answer your question, it's got a little ignitor on it that sparks when you press the button to ignite the propane. Like a spark plug."

"Like a spark plug?" Suddenly I was very interested.

"Yep. Looks like one, too, kind of, only not so high-tech. It's a little ceramic thing, with a wire coming out the end. Doesn't use batteries, either."

I made a mental note to call Theo first thing in the morning.

A final round of coffee and pie was poured and served, and Pastor Stevens tried to open me up again.

"So, Mr. Beckman, I understand you have another mystery going on at the park."

"Another one?"

"I told him about Everett and that other deal," Mr. Curran explained. "I hope that's all right."

I nodded and shrugged. "The police are trying to sort it out, Pastor."

"Estelle told me God has gifted you with the ability to solve mysteries."

I chuckled. "Well, I don't know if it's a gift, as such. It's more a knack, and I certainly don't have an exclusive on it. But whatever you call it, whatever abilities I have, God gave them to me. I guess that makes it a gift. I just never thought of it in the spiritual sense."

"Are you going to solve this one? I mean, are you going to try?"

"Not really. This one's a little out of my league."

Sally had come back into the room after clearing the plates.

"Don't let him kid you," she told the pastor. "He's doing everything he can to figure out who sabotaged the ride. He can't stand to let the police detective get the best of him."

"Not true," I countered. "I just don't like to be told I can't do something."

"A human trait indeed," Pastor Stevens said. "That's why God giving the Israelites the Ten Commandments created such a stir. They immediately wanted to go out and do what He told them they couldn't, and we've been doing the same ever since."

"That's not exactly what I meant," I said in my defense. "I don't do it out of rebellion.

Captain Fitzgerald at the P.D., who will remain nameless, just doesn't like being shown up, so he wants me to keep my nose out of what he considers to be police business. He's afraid I'll solve it before the P.D. and make them look bad."

"And you're bound and determined to do just that," Sally said, tempering it somewhat by saying it softly. "Sounds like rebellion to me."

"Okay," I said with a grin. "Maybe it's rebellion. But it's not rebellion for rebellion's sake. My purpose is not to show them up, although if I do that's okay with me. My purpose is to find out what happened. Let's face it, it's not just police business. Every one of these recent events has involved the park, and I work at the park. I can help with the investigation because of my connections and expertise there. In fact, the lieutenant in charge of the investigations asked me to help him."

"You must have a guilty conscience," Stevens suggested, probably to get back at me for having had fun with his long-winded prayer. "Sounds as if you're trying really hard to justify your involvement."

"No, not at all. Not to myself, anyway, just to my detractors." I gave Sally a look of playful disdain and she smiled sheepishly. "I do it because I like it. In this case, though, I don't really know what to do. I mean, no one was killed, I don't know much about bombs. . . ." I suddenly remembered what Sally had said earlier and shifted gears, looking directly at her.

"Do you really think I've been trying to show Theo up?"

"That's not what I said," Sally replied. "I said you can't stand to let him get the best of you. There's a difference."

I thought about that. The way she put it made it sound bad, but maybe she was right, maybe I did have a motive other than just trying to get to the bottom of things. Maybe I wanted to show Theo — and the whole police department — that I was the best, that they really needed to have me back. But they hadn't gotten rid of me, I had quit. What was I trying to prove?

On the other hand, should I just ignore things, let them handle it when I could really help? Should I not pursue what I enjoy doing, just to avoid appearances? This was not an easy issue, and it's one that I hadn't considered. But Sally had.

"You really think it's a competitive thing?" I asked her. "I mean, really?"

Stevens spoke up. "Competition isn't always a negative thing. It brings out the best

in people sometimes. What you have to consider is — and I'm in no way suggesting
you're guilty of these things . . . I don't even
know you — what are your motives? Do you
revel in your victories? Are you seeking brag-
ging rights? Do you want to *stick it in their
face,* as it were?"

I had to smile. "Probably," I admitted.

"Well, maybe you should do some self-ex-
amination," Stevens suggested, then hur-
riedly added, "We all should from time to
time. It's easy to get caught up in something,
whether it's a cause or an activity, however
noble it might be, that can turn into an obsession. The activity can be right, in itself,
but wrong methods or motives make the activity wrong."

"Gil," said Harold, rising to my defense,
"I don't think your motives are wrong. When
Everett was killed, your goal was to find the
person who did it. I don't think there was
anything in it for you, and I don't think you
considered yourself."

"That's right," agreed Estelle. "And the
other time, when that man was shooting at
you, you would have backed off if you were
only going after him to prove a point,
wouldn't you? You weren't thinking of yourself then."

I shrugged. "I guess not. Well, anyway, it's

my problem to work out. Who's next?" I was beginning to get a little uncomfortable. I don't like public praise any more than I like public criticism. The bottom line was, I did what I did because I felt I had to. That's all there was to it.

There was a strained silence as everyone sat there, feeling a little bad that they had made me the object of their amateur psycho-analysis and wondering what they could say to get out of it. I decided to do it for them by changing the focus.

"So do you all want to know what I've found out so far, or not?"

"Oh, please," said Estelle.

"Yes," echoed Harold.

"That's it, feed his obsession," joked Sally.

"I haven't found out much, folks. I think there might be some connection with Mr. Hiromoto, the Japanese industrialist who's coming to the park Saturday, but I can't pin it down. There's a chance Michelle's friend, one of our landscapers, might be involved. His mother was interned at Manzanar during the war with Michelle's parents."

"Oh, yeah, I know about that place," Harold Curran said. "It's on Highway 395, halfway to the lake. We pass it every time we go up there."

"It's still there?" Sally asked.

"Well, there's not much left. Two guard shacks near the road, the cemetery out behind some trees, and the gymnasium is now the home for the county public works department, or something like that. They use it to house heavy equipment."

"But if you want to find out more about it," Estelle offered, "there's a nice little museum in Independence that's full of things from Manzanar. In fact, if memory serves me right, this weekend is the annual pilgrimage."

"Pilgrimage?" I said.

"Oh, yes. Hundreds of Japanese people who lived in Manzanar return there every year to remember."

I looked at Sally with expectant eyes. "Think you can get a day off?" I asked.

"Now? With Mr. Hiromoto coming? What for? Come on now, Gil, I doubt —"

"Call Harry. Tell him it's real important. Don't tell him where we're going, but tell him it's something I need to do to get ready for the Hiromotos, and I need you to help me."

"You call him. You're the man."

"Yes, but he doesn't mind telling me to go jump in the lake. You, he wouldn't refuse."

"Oh, all right, if you think it's necessary. Just what do you hope to find?"

"How should I know? Maybe the solution

to the mysterious landscaper, maybe nothing. At least it'll be a nice day off, if nothing else. Oh, and . . . uh, by the way. Can we take your car?"

"I knew that was coming," Sally muttered. "Here we go again."

Twelve

We set out early, well before sunup, with an ice chest full of fruit, sandwiches, sodas, cookies, and of course, Pop Tarts, the frosted-brown sugar-cinnamon kind, plus a large thermos of black coffee. Barring any problems, we'd arrive in Independence around 10 A.M., just as the museum was opening.

Keeping Sally's Toyota hovering just over the 55 mark to ward off alien star troopers, we met with very little traffic and hit Lone Pine, about fifteen miles this side of Independence, at 9:30, missing the scenery for the first half of the drive due to darkness, which is just as well because by the time we'd gotten away from the city we were in the desert.

As a rule, I dislike the desert. It's usually hot and dusty and windy and generally inhospitable; but in another sense, I loved it, because walking on the coarse, dry sand in leather-sole shoes made me think of cowboys, and the West, and riding a horse, and sleeping under the stars.

I liked it best, though, when I was driving through it to get somewhere else.

The sky took awhile to get light this morning, hindered by the overcast. Above us, puffy, billowing clouds broke like overstretched taffy, letting invisible shafts of light drop spots of bright color on the ground. The dark silhouette of a line of hills in the distance was obscured by the murky low clouds that dissolved in a torrent of rain onto the parched desert floor. Cumulonimbus clouds several miles off to the east rose like suspended towers resting on glass, inviting amateur photographers to venture out of the comfort of their automobiles for a few snapshots.

Soon rain splattered our windshield, sounding the same as blowing sand but without leaving the pits. The weathered head-frames on top of mine entrances and the blackened skeletons of turn-of-century stamp mills contrasted sharply with the red hillsides they haunted, a reminder of this country's glorious past.

We'd driven past the remains of several long-since extinct volcanoes, now just smooth, vermilion, cone-shaped mounds of barbecue rocks. There were hills and long valleys as far as we could see, everything covered with sparse sagebrush and occasional Joshua trees, except the dry Owens Lake, that spread out over the valley like a beige blanket, clean-shaven by the wind. The closer we drew to Lone Pine the more scenic it became, as the Sierra Nevada mountains rose to our left. Once in Lone Pine proper we could see Mount Whitney's craggy peaks, the highest spot in the continental United States, great splinters of rock pointed skyward.

They were visible only because the weather had begun to clear and the air was warming, and I anticipated a hot day after all.

Lone Pine is the home of the famous Alabama Hills, where multitudes of movies and television shows have been filmed, such as *Gunga Din*, *Khyber Rifles*, *Bengal Lancers*, *High Sierra*, *Joe Kidd*, even a scene from *Chaplin*, and many of the westerns from the 40s and 50s. I wanted to see them, walk through the same hills as Gene Autry, Hopalong Cassidy, John Wayne, and Clint Eastwood, but I didn't have time this trip. Maybe we could stop when I came back by with Harold Curran on our fishing excursion.

We'd already breakfasted on Pop Tarts and coffee and Sally needed a break, so I pulled into a service station that had a mini-mart. I went ahead and filled up the tank, just to save me from having to take the time to do it later.

As I listened to the numbers spinning and the gallons dinging, I stared absentmindedly at some folks in the car on the opposite side of the pump island. Desert travelers, like Sally and myself, dressed much the same with an ice chest in their back seat. I suspected their destination was not much different from ours. In fact, the only meaningful difference between us was our ancestry.

The woman, who had remained seated while the man pumped the gas, kept her eyes straight ahead throughout, her face stoic, a sense of subdued anticipation in her eyes. As her husband replaced the nozzle, her gaze shifted to her rearview mirror, and she caught a glimpse of me out of the corner of her eye. Sensing my scrutiny, she rotated her head toward me, and, as our eyes met, we both smiled uncomfortably, and both turned away.

They drove off, and I finished fueling as Sally returned from the minimart with a box of those chocolate-dipped mini-donuts and some fresh coffee. She looked radiant in her slacks and light sweater, and in the early morning desert sun, I noticed a touch of red in her brown hair I hadn't noticed before. She smiled sweetly — a warm, close friendship smile — that almost embarrassed me. I

225

didn't realize until later that, for the first time, I hadn't thought of Rachel while looking at Sally with any intensity.

We settled back in and hit the road one more time, devouring the coffee and donuts and chatting excitedly about what we'd find. Sally wondered aloud what I was looking for, what Manzanar had to do with all the business going on at the park.

"I don't know, Sal." I sucked some air in with the coffee to cool it. "Ozawa's parents were in Manzanar — his mother at least. Since he's a suspect, it's standard operating procedure to check his background, see if there's some connection between him and the victim —"

"Hiromoto was the victim?" Sally asked. "How did you decide that?"

"We didn't, actually. If George Ozawa is responsible for bombing the Dragon, it's possible it had something to do with the upcoming visit of Hiromoto."

"Why? Just because they're both Japanese?"

"I know, it sounds bigoted. But I don't have any other theories. Not a one." I smiled. "Besides, I thought it'd be fun to take a road trip, you know?"

"Let's hope it's a little less exciting than the last one."

"Could you hand me another donut? . . . Thanks."

"You want me to drive so you can sit here and eat?"

"Mmflgmfl."

"I'm sorry?"

I swallowed. "No thanks. I used to be a cop, remember? I can drive, eat a donut, talk on the radio, hold coffee without spilling it, operate a spotlight . . . all at the same time."

"My hero."

We drove on. Independence was just minutes away when I caught sight of a large, green barn about a quarter mile ahead to our left and well back off the highway.

"Is that it?" Sally asked, a hint of excitement in her voice.

Before I could answer, I saw the stone guard shack marking the entrance to Manzanar — a small house made of smooth rocks indigenous to the area, with a shingled roof, the ridges of which increased in pitch the closer they got to the peak, reminiscent of a Japanese pagoda.

As we closed in on it, a second one appeared, farther from the road and a little smaller but in the same style. I pulled in and parked the car near the larger stone shack.

"Yes," I said, as we stepped out of the car. "This is it."

Walking around the house slowly and touching the stones that had been in place over fifty years transported me back to that time, but my sense of what it was like was purely of my own imagination, since I knew nothing about it. I hadn't a clue what the second stone shack was for.

On the wood lintel over the west window, in white paint or shoe polish, was roughly written:

HAJI MATO
BLK 26-6-3   1-1-86

I guessed a returning internee had placed it there. What the numbers other than the date meant, I didn't know.

We walked onto the grounds, which from the road appeared to have returned completely to their previously natural state. But now we could clearly see pathways, delineated by rows of smooth rocks like those used to build the guard shacks, concrete steps leading nowhere, small rock and concrete ponds void of water, bare concrete foundations. There had indeed been a city here. To the north, the green county building took on a new significance. Gymnasium, town hall . . . now a repository for heavy equipment.

Fifty years later, it was still standing and

put to good use. A structure built with a degree of permanence, ostensibly for the temporary use by Americans of Japanese descent, relocated — against their will — during the war with Japan. I wondered, what was going through the minds of the people . . . the interned Japanese and the white Americans who put them in this desolate place.

The air was calm, and as we stood still in the midst of what had once been Manzanar, there was, for a moment, no sound whatsoever — no breeze blowing past our ears, no cars on the highway, no far-off jets, no screeching birds of prey, no crunching of tennis shoes on the coarse sand. For a minute or two, I had the sensation of deafness as I strained to hear and in a moment, even in the broad expanse of the valley, I felt confined, claustrophobic, my head constricted, my lungs out of breath. Then a noise, a clanking from the road maintenance yard broke the spell, and I took a breath.

All at once it was normal again, as a camper pulling a boat drove by on the highway and the breeze picked up. Sally took a step.

"Did you feel it?" she asked quietly.

"Yes."

Neither of us said any more about it. There

was nothing to add.

As she peered toward the Sierra Nevadas, the nearest peak that of Mount Williamson, our hands brushed together and instinctively clasped, sending a sensation through me I'll not even attempt to describe, but one I hadn't felt in . . . well, as long as I could remember.

"Where's the cemetery?" Sally asked presently.

"I don't know."

"I think there's a monument marking it. A pointed, white thing. I've seen photos."

"I don't see it," I said. "It would have to be out there, past those trees."

"Those are apple trees, aren't they?" Sally asked.

"I'm sure I don't know. Care to take a walk?"

"Sure."

We headed that way, crisscrossing the sagebrush-covered valley floor, finding with each step more and more evidence of the camp, but most of it just more of the same: rocks lined up to mark pathways, broken pieces of china plates or rusted tin cans.

"Watch out for snakes," I cautioned, and Sally moved closer to me, my comment having had the desired effect.

As we made our way through the trees we

could see the monument, stark white and contrasting mightily with the dark hills behind it. Black Japanese characters recessed into the concrete edifice in a vertical line identified the place and a natural wooden fence, looking relatively new, surrounded the cemetery. A dirt road ran in front of it and wound around the rear of the old gymnasium and back toward the highway, and in a clearing opposite the cemetery several portable outhouses had been set up, apparently in preparation for the pilgrimage the next day.

The cemetery was surprisingly small considering the size of the camp and the conditions under which the people lived. There were a few small monuments, and some of them bore dried flowers and coins scattered on the top surfaces.

"I wonder what it says," Sally mused, gazing up at the monument.

"Probably some deep Oriental philosophy about souls on the search for eternal peace," I guessed.

A soft voice behind us said, "It says 'Memorial Tower.' "

I turned to see the woman from the gas station, standing near us within the cemetery fence, her head slightly bowed. Her husband was near the entrance, placing something on a grave marker. She had tied a large-brimmed woven hat onto her head, the green ribbon in a bow beneath her chin, and I could barely see her eyes.

They were narrow, wrinkled eyes, but her mouth smiled sweetly.

"I apologize. I didn't mean to startle you," she said.

I smiled back, and said, "That's okay."

"The literal translation is 'Consolation Soul Tower' but the concept means 'Memorial.' On the other side the writing says, 'August 1943, For the People of Manzanar.' "

"Thank you," I said. "Does the pilgrimage start today?"

"We always come early to pay personal respects to my husband's mother," she explained. "We will return tomorrow for services with the others. You are too young to have known someone here. We were but twenty when we came to Manzanar. We were married here."

The memory seemed fond to her and I was puzzled. How could a prison camp evoke that kind of response? I was a little uneasy, feeling like an intruder into this woman's bittersweet remembrance. To allay this, or somehow justify our presence, I said, "A woman I work with, her parents were here. They would have been about your age then."

"There were ten thousand people here,

many of them my age. But perhaps I know them. What were their names?"

I realized then I didn't know, and said so. "I only know their daughter's married name. I'm sorry."

"Yes, so am I."

As she began to turn away, I had a thought.

"But there is someone else, perhaps you knew him. Kumi Hiromoto." It was a shot in the dark, and a more reasonable man would not have bothered.

She stopped and turned back toward me with an odd expression on her face.

"You know this man?"

"I've heard of him."

"Yes, I too have heard of him. But it is strange that you would know of him."

"Why is that?"

"He was here only for a short time. He repatriated within a few months of coming to Manzanar, was transferred to Tule Lake with the others who wished to return to Japan, and was sent there in 1942 with the first shipload." She paused, then added, "He was one of the Black Dragons."

Her husband called to her from the gate, a hint of anger in his voice. She turned to acknowledge him, then said, "I am sorry. I must leave. Thank you for visiting Manzanar — and remembering."

We watched them disappear into the old apple orchard to return to their car, which was probably also parked near the stone guard house.

"So he was here," I said, intrigued by the revelation.

"Who — or what — were the Black Dragons?" Sally asked.

"I don't know. But I think it's time for that visit to the museum."

Independence, not much more than a five minute drive from the entrance to Manzanar, is the county seat, and boasts one of those classic courthouses: rectangular in shape, sand colored, with four immense Roman columns along the front bearing ornate capitals, many steps leading to the front doors, and a roof that sat like a top hat with human figures in relief inside the triangle under the eaves of the center section of the roof. The building was so large that it dominated the whole town. In fact, it was the only large building. To say the town was small would be an understatement. The only street with businesses was the main highway that ran through town for no more than a half-mile. The courthouse seemed totally out of place in this desert-like environment.

I say desert-like because the town was rife

with trees and greenery, but once outside the city limits, in any direction, the landscape once again reverts to its natural arid state. And during the summers, when the heat settles like a fog or the wind blows the sand into any exposed orifice, "desert" is the only acceptable term.

Following the directions on the small sign, we turned left at the courthouse and drove three blocks to the end of the street and straight into the museum parking lot.

It was a beige, cinder block building, with a grass park and trout pond on the north side, old farm machinery on the south, and a little Western town display out back.

We eagerly went inside. To our right was the employees area with a lady at her desk, to our left a rack of new books for sale, which I hoped included some on Manzanar, and in front of us a small table on top of which was a guest book and a jar for donations. I signed us in, and Sally pushed a few bills into the jar.

A lady greeted us from her desk.

"Welcome. Feel free to look around, inside and out. Let me know if there's anything I can help you with."

"Thank you," Sally said.

"I'm particularly interested in Manzanar," I told her.

"To your left on the other side of the book rack. That whole section of the building is devoted to Manzanar. In fact, we'll be setting up more displays this afternoon. Temporary ones, just for the weekend. Rare stuff you can't see anywhere else."

"Thanks." I looked at Sally expectantly. "Shall we?"

I was not prepared for what I found. Like most Americans, I knew virtually nothing about the internment camps into which we placed our residents and citizens who were of Japanese descent. I had heard of the camps but only by chance comments of friends and in news reports when Congress voted to give each living person who had been so interned twenty thousand dollars as compensation, some forty-five years after the fact. But history books largely ignored the issue, at least when I was in school.

I had imagined the camps were like those I had seen in *Hogan's Heroes* on television, and in the movies. P.O.W. camps, with several rows of barbed wire fences, guard towers with machine guns and searchlights, wooden buildings, gaunt prisoners milling around outside with nothing to do, armed guards walking German Shepherds and carrying rifles.

The first thing that caught my eye was a

large safe from the Manzanar Bank of America. And I didn't expect to see wooden chairs that had been made in the Manzanar furniture shop. There were photos of uniformed baseball teams, high school girls in majorette costumes, art shows, and talent contests. There was a small rubber tire made from guayule, a rubber substitute used during the war and grown at Manzanar, and a set of golf clubs used on the nine-hole course outside the west fence.

A map showed the livestock pens and vegetable farms outside the south fence. There was a hospital, beauty shop, general store, and dress shop. Manzanar had its own newspaper, butcher shop, high school, and dance band (the Jive Bombers). The smaller rock house at the entrance, I discovered, was manned by the Internal Security Police, Manzanar's Japanese police force.

There had been a garden park inside the compound, built by the Japanese. They planted trees, grass, and built a typical, little arched bridge over the creek that ran through the camp. The materials had come from Yosemite, where a truckload of Japanese workers had been taken for the purpose.

The only difference, apparently, between Manzanar and any other American town, was that all the residents were of one race, and none of them were there of their own free will.

And yet, I was bewildered. What started as outrage over the imprisonment of people solely because of their racial ancestry and choice of residence slowly dissolved into a sense of confusion, part of me thinking that they didn't have it so bad, part of me struggling to remind myself that it was forced, and, therefore, no amount of creature comforts could obviate the injustice.

But I now understood the pilgrimage. For four years or so, Manzanar was not just a prison to these people: It was their home. Some were born there; some died there. For many, it became their primary childhood memory — the place they grew up. People met and fell in love and were married while living in Manzanar. Young men left to join the United States Army, leaving their families behind. Many of them would never return, dying for the only country they ever knew or felt loyalty toward, and many would become war heroes.

The reason for the camps — the justification, that is, given by the government — was to prevent espionage. Remove all those of Japanese descent from critical areas to maintain the security of the nation. Not Germans or Italians, just those with easily identifiable faces.

Oddly enough, Hawaiian Japanese weren't interned because they made up too much of the area's work force, and relocating them would have crippled the economy of the islands. Just how serious could the threat have been, I wondered, if the most critical area wasn't cleared of potential spies?

Interestingly, according to the material in the museum, not a single act of espionage was ever uncovered. No person of Japanese ancestry, even the noncitizens living in this country, was ever charged. To most of those interned at Manzanar and the nine other "Relocation Centers," as they were glibly called, the thought of betraying America to the Japanese was an affront and unconscionable. They were Americans, even those who had been barred from becoming citizens by a Supreme Court decision handed down in the 20s.

Despite my surprise, outrage, compassion, confusion, and sorrow, and despite my education received via the artifacts and photographs displayed in the museum, I had learned nothing that would lead me toward the solution of who had sabotaged the roller coaster, and, perhaps more importantly, why.

I was prepared to accept defeat and head back when Sally called me over to a small display of photographs I had missed.

"Look here," she said, in an excited whisper.

I did so, immediately understanding her emotion.

Graffiti painted on a rock formation outside the camp bore the legend *Black Dragons* in a hurried, awkward scrawl. The brief caption told us that The Black Dragons were a group of Japanese young men in their late teens to early twenties, most of them noncitizens, who were anti-American and had sought to instigate uprisings in the various camps. Failing to do so, and refusing to sign a loyalty oath, most were shipped to the camp at Tule Lake in northern California, and many ultimately repatriated with Japan and were delivered by steamship to the island home of their ancestors, with the approval of the Japanese government.

"Hiromoto was a Black Dragon," I said quietly, "and was repatriated. Ozawa was born right about that same time, so they never could have known each other. It doesn't make sense."

"Maybe Mr. Hiromoto knew Ozawa's parents," Sally suggested.

"They're dead," I explained.

"Ask Mr. Ozawa about it."

"Can't do that, Sally. He's a suspect, of sorts, and isn't likely to tell us anything if he's guilty. If he's innocent, he won't know anything. Besides, that's Theo's department. Anyway, the evidence we have is circumstantial and pretty flimsy at best."

"Didn't you say Michelle's parents knew Ozawa's mother?"

"Yeah, that's right. I wonder if I could talk to them."

"Call Michelle, find out where they live. We can call them."

"Can't hurt to try."

Thirteen

I left Sally in the museum to look through the books and see if she could find anything more that would be helpful. The nearest pay phone was at a gas station on the highway.

I called Theo and told him about the barbecue ignitor, then dialed Michelle's direct number.

"This is Michelle."

"Michelle, Gil."

"How's it going, Gil?"

"Pretty good, actually. Look, I need to ask a favor of you."

"What?"

"I'd like to talk to your parents, if it's okay."

"Whatever for?"

"I need some details about Manzanar, people they might have known there."

"I don't know, Gil. I mean, they don't know you, and Manzanar is a pretty sensitive subject. They'll barely talk to me about it."

"I think they may be able to provide the key to this. I'm not sure, but . . . Michelle, Hiromoto was there. In Manzanar."

"Hiromoto? Are you sure? Gil, he's Japanese."

"So was everyone in Manzanar."

"I mean real Japanese. A citizen. I've heard he fought in the war, on their side."

"Maybe he did. But he was in Manzanar during its first year. He repatriated."

Michelle was quiet.

"Michelle?"

"I'm here."

"Well, can I talk to them? I know this is hard, but it's necessary, if only to rule some things out."

She sighed. "All right, Gil. I'll give you their phone number, but I doubt they're home now. They're on their way to Manzanar for the pilgrimage. They might have left already."

"Do you know where they'd stay? What kind of car do they have? I'll try to find them."

She answered both questions and my heart began beating hard. Based on the vehicle description, I already had found them.

Their car was parked in front of their room at the motel in Lone Pine. I knocked on the door, and Michelle's mother answered. She seemed pleased to see me again, yet confused, and perhaps a little alarmed.

"Mrs. Nishiura?" I asked. Michelle had told me their names. Her face flickered apprehension, so I quickly added, "I'm Gil Beckman, this is Sally Foster. We work with your daughter at the amusement park. In fact, at the cemetery it was your daughter I spoke about. She told us where you were."

"Just a moment, please." She excused herself and shut the door, then reopened it and stepped out, closing it behind her.

"My husband is sleeping," she said. Then she waited for me to explain myself.

"I was wondering if we could talk to you about Manzanar some more . . . about someone in particular who was there with you." I anticipated her puzzled expression and kept going. "I work for security at the park, and I'm a former police detective. We had an incident in the park where a roller coaster was intentionally damaged by someone and several people were hurt, could've been killed."

Mrs. Nishiura was understandably confused. "That's very bad, but what does that have to do with Manzanar?"

"It's kind of complicated. Do you have a few minutes? Can we sit down somewhere?"

"Yes. I suppose that would be all right. Mr. Nishiura will sleep. He's taken his medication."

We walked to the family-style restaurant on the same property as the motel and took a booth in the corner. All of us ordered iced tea.

"I have to confess," I said, stirring lemon into my tea, "I was completely ignorant about Manzanar. We went to the museum, and I was surprised to find out what it was like there. Surprised and confused, because it was totally unlike what I was expecting."

"It affects many people that way," Mrs. Nishiura assured. "You think it would have been terrible there: overcrowding, bare walls, supply shortages, armed guards." She smiled. "The truth is, Mr. Beckman, it was all those things, and more. Especially when we first arrived. The whole plan, to relocate all persons of Japanese descent from the west coast, was concocted in such a hurry that it was begun before things were ready. We were first sent to race tracks up and down the coast where we lived in the horse stables. They whitewashed the walls and gave us very little notice that we were to be packed and were to report to certain locations, sometimes within twenty-four hours. We could only take what we could carry, and no provisions were made to safeguard our property and possessions. Much was sold for a fraction of its value, some was left locked up and promptly looted, some of us managed to let Caucasian friends hold on to our things for us.

"Even with the temporary housing to give them time to build the camps, when we finally made the train and bus trip to Manzanar, the accommodations were not completed. The fence was not even put up, and that work was finished by internees. We built our own fence!" She laughed unashamedly at this irony.

"The housing was in wood and tarpaper barracks, sectioned in blocks. The rooms were bare, with cracks between the boards that let in the wind and the cold and the sand, with too many people per room. We fixed them up as time went on and materials became available, but it was never really comfortable. You could hear everything that went on in your neighbors' rooms."

"What did they do with all your furniture, your things? You say you couldn't take those to Manzanar?"

"We gave what we could to our neighbors to store, but they didn't have room for all of it. Some of it we sold to unscrupulous people who preyed on our fear and gave us less than ten percent of its value."

"Your house, did you lose that?"

"And the car and the land my parents had worked so very hard to buy. We came here from Japan when I was ten, and I had very few memories of the country of my birth. This was to be a new life, a free life. My parents would not even let us speak Japanese in public after we had all learned English. 'You are Americans, little children,' my mother would say. I'm afraid I became very rusty."

"How did being put in the camp affect her?"

"In different ways, but it did not change her loyalty to this, her chosen country. Although unable to become a citizen since a Supreme Court decision in 1922 said that Japanese people could not do so, she considered herself an American, as did I. We made the most of our situation, believing it would work out all right. We even tried to understand why we were there, tried to put ourselves in the place of the whites who were afraid of us because we looked different from them. We could not understand completely, but we realized very soon that it did not matter whether we understood or how we felt about being there. It only mattered that Manzanar was our home, and so we sought to turn it into just that — a home."

She closed her eyes, as if imagining those things that made their barracks room something special.

"Father built a little walkway lined with rocks that led to our front steps. It's still there, you may have seen it. Many people did the same. We also had a vegetable garden and eventually managed to get a hot plate so we could cook our own food on occasion."

"You didn't have kitchens?"

"Oh, no. Each block had its own dining hall, and we had to wait outside in long lines, whatever the weather, to eat. The food, I will admit, was generally good, except when they tried to serve Japanese dishes." She chuckled. "They did not understand rice. They kept trying to dress it up with sweet toppings, like a dessert, to make it more palatable to us, a way we would never eat it. They never realized they were making it more palatable for *themselves*."

"You mentioned shortages."

"Oh, yes, when we first arrived there was not enough food, and little variety. Remember, they weren't really ready for us, but they were panicked and moved very quickly to put us out of harm's way, so to speak. But they quickly improved that aspect of the camp. Other deficiencies took longer."

"Such as?"

"The bathroom facilities. They were large rooms with no privacy, just rows of toilets. The government seemed to suffer from the delusion that we were all related and, therefore, did not know modesty; or that, because we were all of one race, it somehow did not matter. They did have separate facilities for men and women, I'll give them credit for that." She laughed again.

"You seem to have fond memories," I marvelled. "How can that be?"

"Well," she sighed, smiling a bit, her eyes brightening. "I met Mr. Nishiura in Manzanar, for one thing. It was right after I first arrived. He was handsome and strong, with a bright smile. I fell in love immediately, and somehow, he did the same."

I could see how. The more I watched her face as she spoke, the more I could see the resemblance with Michelle.

"Mr. Nishiura, he was Nisei — he was born in the states. If you count from him, Michelle is actually third generation. He volunteered for the army. I didn't want him to go, but he was determined to show his loyalty. He served with the 442nd Battalion in Italy, fighting the Germans, where he won two purple hearts."

"While his family was back home — in a prison camp."

"Relocation Center," she corrected. "That was the official name for it. Whatever the conditions, or our reason for being there, we had committed no crimes and were not in prison. It was against our will, yes, but not entirely so."

"Oh? How's that?"

"We could move East, after a time, if we wanted. The relocation was contested on constitutional grounds, and while the Supreme Court said the army could force us to leave the Pacific coast, which they considered a sensitive area, they could not incarcerate us. It's just that most could not move or were reluctant to do so, thinking they would shortly be returned to their homes and property. And since they were staying, they were subject to the terms: We would live in camps under guard to prevent espionage activity. In retrospect, it was silly, but then there was a great fear, and fear is a difficult thing to overcome."

"How could you do it, Mrs. Nishiura? How could you not just survive but thrive during that time and years later retain such fond memories? Aren't you angry?"

"The Japanese have a word, Mr. Beckman: *giri*. There is no equivalent word in English, but it basically means to respond to a negative situation, while persevering happily. It's also the idea of living up to an obligation. The old saying, 'when life hands you lemons, make lemonade,' gives you an idea what *giri* is. We were there, we could not change that, so we worked hard to turn it into something that was our own. And for many people, it became something important and even comfortable. When it finally came time to leave, many hesitated, reluctant to leave behind the memories, the hard work they had put into the place. It was the only home they had known for four years."

"The battered wife syndrome," I said absentmindedly.

Mrs. Nishiura and Sally both gave me funny looks, so I explained.

"Battered wives frequently will not have their husbands put in jail, because then they would be without monetary support, having to fend for themselves. Fear of the unknown — how to buy food, get shelter, take care of the kids — is stronger than fear of their husband."

"Yes," Mrs. Nishiura said. "But it wasn't so much a fear of leaving as it was an attachment to our new homes. With *giri* there comes also a contentment."

"Something I am trying to learn," I admitted.

"He's doing well, too," Sally offered in my defense. "It's something that everyone needs to learn."

"Yes. That is something the Japanese are

good at. Now tell me, Mr. Beckman. Why did you ask about Kumi Hiromoto? And what does Manzanar have to do with Mr. Hiromoto and the amusement park?"

"He's the founder of Hiro Industries, did you know that?"

"I have heard that."

"He's coming to the park tomorrow. He wants to build one just like it in Nagasaki." She nodded, but said nothing. "So, what can you tell me about him?" I asked.

"Is this very important?"

"It's life or death, Mrs. Nishiura. Perhaps Mr. Hiromoto's."

She nodded reflectively, understanding. "Well . . . as I said, he was a Black Dragon. He tried to stir up trouble in the camp, create a riot, but was unsuccessful. He was sent to Tule Lake, where the troublemakers were all sent. Not everyone in Tule Lake was a troublemaker. They just put them all in one place."

"What about George Ozawa?"

She was a little concerned by this question. "What does he have to do with Mr. Hiromoto?"

"That's what I was hoping you'd tell me."

"They couldn't have known each other. George Ozawa was born in the camp."

Just the way she worded it gave me the

feeling she was hedging. I changed course.

"Did you know George Ozawa's mother well?"

"We were best friends."

"Tell me about his father."

"He went to war with my husband. He was killed in Italy."

"Did Mr. Ozawa's mother know Mr. Hiromoto?"

Mrs. Nishiura dropped her head to prevent her eyes from revealing the truth, but she did not want to lie to me.

"How well, Mrs. Nishiura? How well did she know him?"

She sighed and looked up. "He wanted to marry her, but she would not betray her fiancé, Benny Ozawa, whom she promised to wait for. But Kumi persisted, and she continued to resist. She knew it was wrong, that it could never work, because even then he was in with the Black Dragons, and Sachiko Takada loved America. She would cry to me when we were alone, how he would try to make her hate her country. Benny had only been gone a month when Sachiko came to me, sobbing that she was pregnant. I asked if . . . if Kumi had done this thing to her, if he had raped her, but she would not tell me. She would only cry. A few weeks later Kumi Hiromoto was sent to Tule Lake, and the discussion was closed. I would not pry."

Mrs. Nishiura took a deep breath. "Sachiko eventually told me the father was Benny Ozawa, and I did not question her. She was shamed enough, since they had not married. When we got word that Benny had been killed, she became very withdrawn. But she had the baby and raised him, giving him Benny's name and telling him when he was old enough that his father died bravely in the service of his country so that his son might be free."

"But he wasn't the father, was he," I said softly.

She shook her head. "No. Kumi Hiromoto was. She confessed this to me in her later years, just before she died. To clear her conscience, perhaps. She still did not say whether it was rape or if she had given in to him in a weak moment, but I don't believe it made a difference to her because of the guilt she felt. She should not have entertained his affections at all, and if that was the result, she had no one to blame but herself. Those were her thoughts, not mine."

"Did George ever find out?"

"I didn't tell him, but it is possible his mother did. I saw him the day after she died, and he was a changed man. This was five years ago. He left his job and kept to himself for several months, and when he finally came out of it, he got Michelle to help him get him a job at the park. We have seen very little of him since then."

There was a lull while I tried to make something out of this, then Mrs. Nishiura continued. "There is something else you should know. Despite his shameful act with Sachiko, and his ties with the Black Dragons, Mr. Hiromoto was an honorable man. He tried to make it right. He wrote Sachiko many times, asking her to come to Japan to live with him, to be his wife. She refused to answer the letters, and he eventually gave up. But when their son, George, was ready to enter college, he received a letter from USC telling him that he had been given a scholarship that would pay for his entire college education. We don't know for sure, but we suspect it came from Mr. Hiromoto."

There the story ended as she abruptly fell silent. Mr. Nishiura had entered the restaurant.

He looked around and located his wife, then walked to our table with a dour face. I stood up and introduced myself and Sally, explaining that we worked with his daughter and were appreciative of his wife's hospitality in helping us understand Manzanar. I said nothing specific to him because I perceived a sense of distrust on his part. Mrs. Nishiura had contributed to this with her clandestine meeting while her husband slept and her clamming up when he appeared. Whether it was because he was distrustful of strangers, or because the internment was highly personal, or a bad memory, I would never know.

He was abrupt but cordial and acknowledged my gratitude.

"Mrs. Nishiura, you've been very helpful," I said. "I appreciate your candor and enjoyed hearing about Manzanar from someone who was there. I'll never forget it and would ask that maybe someday you could tell me more."

She smiled shyly, and said, "Will you be staying for the ceremonies tomorrow?"

"I wish we could, but I've got to escort Mr. — I've got to go to work in the morning."

Her eyes told me she had given me the information in confidence, and I tried to tell her with mine that I understood. I hoped she got the message.

We got up, and I left a five on the table. I thanked them both again before Sally and I left the restaurant and piled in the car for the return trip.

"What do you think?" she asked as we

pulled out onto the highway.

"I think," I said slowly, "I think I better call Theo and tell him Mr. Ozawa is going to try to kill Mr. Hiromoto."

Fourteen

We drove home, stopping only once to get some dinner at a middle-of-nowhere ranch house-style eatery. It was packed, being the only place for miles in either direction.

Theo had argued that Ozawa should be brought in and questioned, what with motive, opportunity, and the circumstantial evidence all piled on top of it like grated cheese on chili. He even thought that charges might be filed if he could induce Ozawa to cop out.

The problem, he explained, is the difficulty of convincing a D.A. to stick his neck out and charge Ozawa with sabotage — attempted murder as well — when his motive apparently involved a man who wasn't present. It would be a hard sell to the jury, twelve normal people (who don't read newspapers or watch TV news).

"Get a confession," I told him, "I'd be able to."

"Yeah, right," Theo had said. "A claim you can't prove."

"Nor could you disprove," I said and hung up.

It was late when we got back, and I took the sleepy Sally home, taking her car with me. She'd picked me up, but I didn't feel good letting her drive home alone. I'd come back in the morning to take her to the park with me.

I decided to run by the park before I went home to bed, to see if there were any last minute details I could attend to and also to check with security on who was scheduled to work. My hope was that all days off had been cancelled.

The light was on in Harry's office, which was not a big surprise. Managers took turns working as on-duty park supervisor, and Friday was Harry's night. And with all the goings-on in the morning, I'd've been surprised if he wasn't there anyway.

I tapped on the door, and he told me to come in.

"Oh, it's you," he said. "How'd it go?"

"Okay, I guess. I think we may have our culprit."

"I heard. They picked Ozawa up when he left work this afternoon. At least that's something we don't have to worry about."

"If he's the real culprit."

"Second thoughts?"

"No, I'm just not absolutely sure. This airtight case has too many holes in the top of the can."

"Well, it should be all right tomorrow, in any case. We've covered all the bases."

"Yeah."

There was an awkward silence while I waited for Harry to bring up the subject, but, true to form, he was avoiding giving me the unpleasant news. I couldn't wait, so I asked him outright.

"Harry."

"Yes?" He looked up from the papers he'd gone back to flipping through.

I hesitated, then said, "I understand I'm back in security now, full time. Could you give me a few details?"

"Huh? Oh, yes. I . . . uh . . . we haven't worked it out completely. We'll know more next week."

"What's to work out? Where will I be assigned? Just give me a hint, okay?"

"I can't until it's official."

"Harry, I'm not a kid. You can't bluff me. And I can take bad news. You don't need to protect me. In fact, I expect bad news. What's my new assignment?"

"I . . . I expect you'll be placed in a position that will most utilize your experience and abilities."

Management double-talk. "Oh," I said, "why didn't you say so?" The truth was,

Harry was handing me a line of claptrap. Somebody else was pulling his strings so confronting him was pointless. Entertaining, perhaps, but pointless. Poor Harry. Maybe he'd be better at running his department if they'd let him run the department. Then again, maybe not.

You'll be placed. What did that tell me, I thought sarcastically. Obviously, someone was giving Harry orders, at least regarding my future. The question was, who? Jerry Opperman? Michelle? One of the owners? Maybe Captain Fitzgerald from the P.D. was influencing Harry. Fitzgerald never did like me and had Harry's ear whenever he wanted it.

Just to return to security at all was bad news, and Harry's reluctance to commit told me I was undoubtedly going back into uniform. Probably graveyard. Oh well, at least I was employed.

Effectively getting the answer to my question, I stood up and told Harry I'd see him in the morning. He grunted, happy to be off the hook, then waved me off and went back to his papers.

I went to the report writing room, which was empty of people, and phoned the P.D. Theo was still there and in a moment — after I listened to two minutes of Tony Bennett while on hold — my ex-partner came on the line.

"Lieutenant Brown."

"Evening, Theo. Would you mind putting me back on hold? The song wasn't over."

"Don't tell me, let me guess. Gil Beckman. Am I right?"

"Close enough for government work. So how'd it go? Is this a done deal? Did you extract a confession out of the recalcitrant suspect? Leave him puddled on the floor in a bubbling mass of divulgence? Did Ozawa sing, spill his guts, cop out, snitch himself off?"

"No."

"Excuse me, which question were you answering?"

"All of them."

"Couldn't get him to give it up, eh?"

"He refused to talk."

"Invoked his right to silence, or just wouldn't confess to the crime?"

"No, he didn't invoke. He said he'd cooperate fully. But he denied knowing anything about it."

"What did he admit?"

"To his name, his position at the park. That's about it."

"What about Hiromoto?"

"When I asked Ozawa if he knew him, the

gardener shook his head and clammed up and asked for an attorney. That was the end of that."

"So you never got into the Manzanar connection?"

"Nope."

"Any problem with Michelle on the arrest?" I asked tentatively.

"I don't know," Theo said with a chuckle. "She won't talk to me."

"Seems like this isn't your day for striking up conversations. She'll be madder at me, probably. I haven't seen her yet." When I said this, I thought back to my conversation with Harry. Maybe Michelle was indeed behind my probable return to uniforms. After all, she took me out of them. I thought we had a good relationship, but had I crossed the line? Ozawa wasn't a blood relative of hers but might as well have been.

"What did you find out about the barbecue thing? The ignitor."

"That looks like what was used. The piece we have corresponds to what we found at the store. I asked Ozawa if he had a barbecue, and he said he did, gave me permission to go look, and —"

"His ignitor was missing."

"You got it. During the questioning he did say he bought the barbecue at a yard sale, and the ignitor worked the last time he used it."

"When was that?"

"Six months ago."

"Did it look like it'd been that long?"

"Yeah, I suppose. It was clean, but dusty."

"Another brick in the evidence wall."

"Circumstantial," Theo reminded me. "Like all the others. But every little bit helps."

"Where is his barbecue?"

"In the backyard, of course."

"How accessible is it? You know, could someone jump over the rear fence easily?"

"I suppose. Why?"

"I don't know. Just wondering. What are the chances of getting the D.A. to file?"

"Without a cop-out? Slim to none without more concrete evidence."

"Are you going to let him go?"

"We'll have to if the D.A. doesn't cooperate. Since it's a weekend, we can keep him until Monday noon. After that, if we don't formally charge him, he walks."

"That's okay. We'd like him to stay at least until the Hiromotos are gone tomorrow evening. That'll work."

"I'll do what I can, but if he bails before then, he bails. He has no record, but he won't get released on his own recognizance.

Bail is $25,000, and he told me he couldn't raise it."

"What's your plan if he manages to get out early? Do you have someone who can tail him, at least until the Hiromotos are gone?"

"Yeah, the narcs aren't busy right now. If Ozawa goes home — and there's no reason to believe he'll do anything else now that he knows we know what's going on — I'll have someone babysit him until things at the park are clear."

"Okay. Sounds good. Sorry I couldn't be there to get the confession for you."

"Breaks my heart, Columbo."

I set the receiver down easily on the cradle and went out into the cool, misty night, tired from the day of travel and discovery, anxious for a good night's sleep. I would be glad when tomorrow was over.

The next morning I found Harry in the security squad room amidst the chaos of uniformed and plainclothes security officers. Sally had retreated to her office to attend to some last minute detail and would join me momentarily.

The park wouldn't open for another hour — and Hiromoto wasn't due for two — but Harry already looked stressed.

And lost. Standing in the center of the

room, his eyes vacant, he was the only person not in motion. Like the vortex of a black hole or the center of a cyclone, Harry Clark anchored the swirling mass of humanity that meandered in apparent aimlessness about him. It was not only an interesting visual, it was an accurate picture of the way his department functioned under his leadership.

I picked my way through the men and women and greeted the security chief.

"Well, are we ready?" I asked.

"I hope so. The assignments are written. We'll hand them out in a few minutes when we have briefing. Where's your suit and tie?"

"At home in a heap on the floor. After the other day, I needed to have them cleaned."

"What I mean is, why aren't you wearing one?"

"Eric Hiromoto said they want to look inconspicuous. If I'm going to escort them and walk around in the sun all day, I'm going to blend in. You have a hostess assigned to them?"

"Not yet. I thought I'd ask Sally to do it, if that's okay with you."

My initial reaction was negative, especially since the threat of danger was present — however remote it might have been — but when I thought about it, I decided I'd rather spend the day with Sally than with some young lady I didn't know. Besides, I'd be there to keep an eye on her, and I knew if something happened I could count on her to respond immediately to whatever I asked her to do.

"Sure, Harry, that's fine with me. I'm sure she'd be happy to oblige."

"Good. Jerry will be here shortly, to —"

"Jerry? Jerry Opperman?"

"Of course, Gil. What did you think? He's the president, for goodness' sake. What did you expect?"

"I guess I just forgot about him, that's all."

"This is his deal, Gil. It would be insulting for him not to show — probably blow the whole deal."

I didn't know which would be worse: Jerry not showing and insulting the Hiromotos, or Jerry showing up and insulting them all day with his weirdness. Oh, well. There was nothing I could do but make the best of it and try to keep the Hiromotos busy.

"You ready to start?" I asked.

"Yes."

"Okay." I banged on the table. "Okay, people. Listen up. Find a seat or a comfortable place to stand."

The milling slowed as people dropped into chairs or grabbed a piece of wall, then the dayshift sergeant passed around the assignment sheets and special information. There was some murmuring as the folks considered their assignments — and a few grumbles.

"No trading," I told them. "We set it up like we did for a purpose." I hadn't a clue what that was, since Harry had done it all by himself without consulting me, but it sounded good. It won me a point with Harry, too, which is the real reason I said it. I turned the meeting over to Harry.

For the next fifteen minutes he droned on about such things as business as usual, don't draw attention to the V.I.P.s, stay sharp, don't tell other guests who they are or why they're here, monitor your radios, blah blah blah. I listened with one ear, already knowing what I would need to do, and reflected on Manzanar, the bombing of the Dragon, George Ozawa, Kumi Hiromoto and his grandson. . . . I replayed the whole scenario over and over again in my mind. Something was bothering me, but I just couldn't put my finger on it.

Harry told us that after the park closed last night, the P.D. went through it with a bomb dog, and everything checked clean. The Dragon would be operating. The track had been given a clean bill of health, as had the back-up cart string.

Management would be out in force, Harry

told us. So would administration. Not just Jerry Opperman, but the department heads, vice presidents, and maybe even the owners.

In other words, a fiasco, a circus, a dog-and-pony show. So much for a normal day at the amusement park and remaining inconspicuous.

Sally came into the room midway through the briefing. I gave her a wink. She smiled and found a seat in dispatch where she could still hear what Harry was saying.

Harry delivered final instructions — including, "Everyone act like nothing's different from normal." I shook my head. That's like shouting "Don't look!" to a crowd of people. He fielded a few questions before dismissing us with a comment designed to appeal to our loyalty and ego, then everyone filed out.

I met Sally outside the rear door, in the backstage area.

"We've got some time," I said. "Want to get some breakfast?"

"Okay," she said. She looked up at me with doe eyes. I'd seen them before some months back, just prior to having to fight for my life. I smiled back at her, remembering that moment, but didn't let her mesmerize me, looking away before I became too self-conscious.

"Then I'll take you to the park for a day," I told her. "My treat."

She hooked her hand in the crook of my elbow and looked up at me, batting her eyes.

"Big spender," she cooed.

Fifteen

The employee cafeteria was serving fresh croissant rolls and blueberry muffins. We drew some coffee, got a plate of muffins, and found a table. I had a radio with me, earphone attached, and monitored dispatch, just in case Hiromoto decided to come early, which wouldn't have surprised me. We told him to come in via the receiving gate to avoid having to deal with the crowd outside at the ticket booths and to park his car by security. From there, we'd take him into the park through one of the employee gates. Once inside, we'd blend.

Sally took a dainty bite of her muffin with a fork. She watched me as she chewed, her mouth barely moving.

"What?" I said when I became aware of her scrutiny.

She blushed. "Sorry." She offered no explanation and returned to her muffin. Presently she spoke.

"You're sure taking it well. I'm proud of you."

"Taking what well?"

"Coming back to security."

I exhaled. "I'm not taking it as well as I'm letting on," I admitted. "But I realize several things. Number one, God's in control. Not Harry Clark, not Gil Beckman, not Jerry Opperman. Especially not Jerry Opperman. Number two, there's nothing I can do about it."

"You could leave."

"And go where?" I shrugged. "Besides, I knew all along it would happen sooner or later, which is point number three. I knew this assignment was temporary. I'm not saying I won't miss it — on several levels — and I'm certainly not happy about it. But . . . what else can I say?"

"Well, I'm glad you feel that way," Sally said.

"Me too. Nothing else would be productive."

She asked about Ozawa, what Theo had found out. I gave her the rundown on it.

"You don't sound happy," she observed, rightly.

"There's just something about the whole thing that . . . I don't know what it is. It's like I'm looking at a puzzle. I can see enough of it to see what the picture is, but there's still some big holes in it, that when they're filled in will change the final picture into something different than what I see now. Basically the same, perhaps, but different. Does that make any sense?"

"Kind of. You don't think Ozawa did it?"

"He has the motive — the shaming of his mother by Hiromoto — the opportunity with Hiromoto coming here, access to explosives, the technical knowledge, his barbecue is missing its ignitor. . . ."

"But you're not convinced."

I leaned back in my chair. "No, I'm not. And I don't know why."

"Maybe God is giving you some uneasiness about it to make you look deeper."

"Look deeper where? We have no other leads, whatsoever. Everything points to Ozawa. You know," I said slowly, "that's what bothers me. Everything points to Ozawa, except his character. I know, I know, you can't always judge by that. Like that baseball player who blew his ex-wife away with a shotgun and tried to make it look like a suicide. Nobody wanted to believe he did it, but it happened."

I polished off my coffee. "But even if Ozawa did it, there's still problems. I can't make sense out of the small amount of explosives and the premature discharge."

"I thought you had decided he was just testing it."

"Yeah, I theorized that. But why? If he wanted to kill Hiromoto why not just put a pipe bomb on it and blow it to kingdom come? He could test the electronics of the device at home without explosives attached. And why risk premature discovery with an unnecessary test? Besides, an incident on the ride like that might have caused Hiromoto to change his mind, to not show up at all."

"Then he was trying to derail the business deal," Sally suggested.

"If Ozawa's motive was revenge — or avenging his mother — that wouldn't accomplish anything. Hiromoto's not going to lose anything by calling the deal off, the park is."

"Maybe he's working with someone else who would benefit," Sally said.

I shook my head. "Doesn't make sense. Who would benefit from Hiromoto backing out?" It was a rhetorical question at this point, since neither Sally nor I had a clue.

"But how could Ozawa know Mr. Hiromoto would ride the Dragon?"

"That's just it," I said. "That's what's bothering me. How could he know?"

Any further conversation would have to wait. My earphone hissed and the dispatcher's dispassionate voice called my radio number.

"Security Four," I responded into the remote microphone at the end of my shirt cuff. The wire ran up inside my sleeve and down into the small radio clipped to my belt.

"Receiving gate reports Guest is on scene. Limo just drove past his booth."

"Ten-four." I looked at Sally, who couldn't hear what I'd been told. "The rest of our party has arrived. Shall we?" I offered my arm as I stood.

We walked to security, passing Hiromoto's white stretch limo, and headed for the conference room. They were already inside.

Kumi Hiromoto was a small man, but stood erect and proud, his face set in a permanent grin, his nose unencumbered by glasses. He spoke only in hushed tones to his interpreter, bowing with each introduction then extending his hand American-style. He wore a sport shirt and casual pants, with new leather Nike shoes on his feet and a white straw Panama on his head. It was hard to believe this man was worth millions upon millions, but, then again, what did a millionaire look like? And should they act any different than anyone else when they spend a day at the theme park?

Eric Hiromoto, on the other hand, was dressed much the same as he was the day I met him at his office, only his suit coat had been replaced by an unnecessary black leather jacket, and he had added a pair of designer sunglasses, which hung by a cord from his neck. The bespectacled interpreter, introduced as Toyo Wakigama, dressed casually and unobtrusively, with clothing I might have picked out for myself — only smaller — but he appeared uncomfortable nonetheless. Maybe it had nothing to do with the clothes but the situation itself.

The large man was Toshi. That's all, just Toshi. I think that must be the Japanese equivalent for Guido. He was so obviously a bodyguard that I doubted the camera around his neck even contained any film, and he stood behind the Hiromotos with his hands clasped together in front of him, glaring at each of us in turn, as if trying to read our intentions toward his boss, to discover if any of us were threats, or perhaps just to intimidate us. When he caught my eye I gave him a flirtatious wink to counter his officiousness and let him know I was unmoved by his demeanor. I'm quite sure he determined then and there to keep a wary eye on me. He looked hot in his heavy coat. In fact, only the elder Hiromoto was properly dressed for the occasion. Someone forgot to tell them this was mostly outdoors.

Kumi Hiromoto spoke to his interpreter in whispered but audible Japanese, and the interpreter relayed the entrepreneur's request.

"Mr. Hiromoto wants to know when he will meet Everett. He is very anxious to shake hands with the dinosaur who captured the armed criminal."

"I'm anxious to see that myself," I muttered to Sally.

"We have arranged for that meeting around noon," Harry told them. "As soon as you are in the vicinity of the main gate, he'll be there."

"The main gate?" Eric Hiromoto asked. "We would prefer a private meeting. My grandfather would like to extend his personal congratulations and ask the dinosaur how he managed it."

I grinned at Harry's discomfort. The first major snag.

"Uh . . . I . . . don't know if we can arrange —"

"What Harry's trying to say, Mr. Hiromoto," I interjected, "is that Everett doesn't talk. He is, after all, a dinosaur. I'm sure Mr. Hiromoto can understand that."

The interpreter mumbled, and Hiromoto the elder responded.

"He says he understands that Everett is just a costume," Mr. Wakigama said. "He wants to talk to the brave person who was wearing the suit."

"The problem is," Harry said slowly, "we have more than one person who portrays Everett. At any one time there might be three, all in different areas of the park." I had forgotten that Harry didn't know who was in the suit at the robbery. No one had told him it was me.

"Mr. Hiromoto will be very disappointed if he cannot meet the correct Everett. That is one of the main reasons he came here."

"Don't worry," I said. "He'll be there, whenever you're ready. I can contact him."

Wakigama translated then repeated Hiromoto's response while the elderly man smiled. "He says, like Clark Kent and Superman."

I laughed and nodded. "Right. Just like Clark Kent."

Sally suppressed a chuckle and said under her breath, "Not quite, big guy."

We reviewed the order of business one more time then left Security to make our way directly to the stage door entrance we were to use. We would beat the general opening of the park by about ten minutes, giving the Hiromotos the opportunity to ride the attraction they wanted to the most before anyone else got to it. They — Eric Hiromoto, that is — had expressly requested that they not be given special consideration when it came to standing in line so as not to attract undue attention or irritate any of the other customers. I suggested that, considering the makeup of our little band, there was no way we could go all day and not attract some attention, unless we managed to lose the big guy, Toshi.

"Tell him to lighten up," I suggested to Eric. "He's a little overbearing with his evil-eye routine and the way he hunches his shoulders every time someone approaches, like a gorilla protecting his mate with intimidation. He might as well walk around with his hand inside his coat so he can draw that hogleg out of his shoulder holster quickly."

"He's not armed," Eric Hiromoto said.

"Care to let me check?" I asked.

Harry broke in. "That won't be necessary, Gil. He's fine, Mr. Hiromoto. Just fine. Now shall we go?"

The interpreter gave Kumi Hiromoto a running account of the conversation. Kumi just listened without reacting but gave me several serious looks.

They filed out the door, and Harry grabbed me by the sleeve and drew me back into the hallway.

"What are you trying to do, embarrass us? Don't push these people."

"That guy is armed, Harry, and you know

it. That's illegal. Do you want him running around this amusement park shooting the first idiot that gets pushy in a line?"

"Well, we can't prove he's armed," Harry hedged.

"You can see it poking out from under his arm in the back."

Harry ignored me. "Besides, this is private property and I'm sure the owners would choose to overlook it, since Mr. Hiromoto is so. . . ." He couldn't tell me what Mr. Hiromoto was but decided instead to pull rank. "Just go with them and do your job. And don't tick off Jerry. Remember, Gil, he's the head man around here."

I wanted to do something with that line but restrained myself. "You're right, Harry." There was nothing else to say. I turned to leave, but before I made it to the door the phone rang, and the dispatcher hailed me.

"It's for you, Gil. Lieutenant Brown."

"Okay. I'll take it in the report writing room."

I picked up the receiver when the call was transferred. "Theo? Gil here. What's up?"

"He's out," Theo said abruptly.

"Ozawa?"

"Yep. Posted bail. Or rather, had bail posted for him."

"By whom?"

"Bail bondsman. He wouldn't say who arranged for it."

"Could it have been Michelle?"

"That's my guess, but since we're not talking, I have no way of knowing."

"Sorry, Theo. I didn't think about that before I got into this."

"That's the way it goes, I guess," Theo sighed. "I can't let personal relationships affect my work."

"What are you going to do now?"

"I'm having him tailed, to make sure he doesn't go to the park. They just called in and said he went straight home."

"Okay. Well, keep me posted. Oh, by the way, did you find out anything on that fingerprint?"

"It's not Ozawa's, but there were others that were too smudged to be recognizable. That it wasn't his doesn't prove he didn't do it."

"Whose was it?"

"Don't know yet. Everybody checked clear but that sweeper. We couldn't get him in for prints."

"He refused to come in?"

"No, the address Sally gave us was no good."

"He moved?"

"Doesn't exist. Maybe you can check it

again, see if she got it wrong."

"I doubt that. Did you check the Department of Motor Vehicles?"

"No license issued. But that isn't conclusive since the name he gave the park might be slightly different from his legal name. A lot of times they use American first names. Didn't his name tag say Joe?"

"Yeah. I'll check park records again," I said, "just to make sure, and I'll get back to you this morning. The Hiromotos are here, and I have to get going. Page me if you need anything. I'll call you from a pay phone out in the park."

"Ten-four, good buddy."

We rang off, and I hurried outside to catch up to my guests.

They were just entering the park, and Sally was looking behind them for me. She relaxed visibly when I appeared and waved to hurry me up. There were whispers between Elder and the interpreter, who then turned to scold me.

"Mr. Hiromoto says to please remain with us today and do not lag behind."

I said nothing but nodded assent, yielding to the distinguished guest.

We went first to Moonraiders. As we entered the ride, Sally and I stepped back and went around to the exit to wait for them. At first she wondered why but didn't say anything. I knew she was puzzled because of the look on her face. When we were alone, I explained.

"In the first place, we can't even see them while the ride is in progress, so what good is that? Second, I want to be there waiting when they get off. Besides, if there should somehow be an explosive on the ride, I'd rather be out here. The Dragon bomb was set off remotely, and I want to be where I can see who's doing it. You and me getting blown up won't help Hiromoto. And no, I don't think there's a bomb anywhere in there. I'm just being cautious."

I didn't tell her that Ozawa was out of jail.

"Where's Mr. Opperman?" Sally asked, but she immediately answered her own question. "Oh, here he comes. Looks like Miss Yokoyama is with him. Oh my, she doesn't look very happy."

"Where are they, Buckner?" Jerry asked in a huff when he reached us.

"Inside, having fun. They'll be out in no time."

"Aren't you supposed to be in there with them?"

I shrugged. "Too dark to see anything. I thought it'd be better to stay out here and keep watch." I turned my attention to

Michelle. "Miss Yokoyama. How are you today?"

She forced a weak smile. "Fine." It faded instantly.

"I appreciate how you feel, Michelle," I said. "Honest, I do. And I hope we're wrong. But have you heard the evidence?"

"No, and it doesn't matter. I know he wouldn't do that."

"Well, you have the benefit of knowing him very well. But Theo and I are forced to look at the evidence and leave our feelings out of it."

"Maybe you should listen to your feelings sometime."

"What's this all about?" Opperman asked.

"Nothing," Michelle said and turned away just as our guests came down the exit ramp.

None of them were aware we hadn't been on the ride with them. They were too enthralled with their trip to the moon. Kumi grinned like a kid and chattered with Waki, as I had begun to call him (to myself). Eric seemed pleased, but his delight was stifled by his pompousness. Toshi had broken a sweat. Kumi greeted Jerry and Michelle like they were old friends.

Next stop was the nearby Dinosaur Kingdom. Normally, Everett could be found wandering around outside, greeting the kids and hugging their mothers, but with the park just now due to open, he hadn't arrived. He began his shift an hour after opening, to give the place time to fill up.

We hiked up the ramp, Sally and I to the front, Toshi playing caboose, and climbed into the nonstop carts from the moving ramp to be transported back to the Plasticene Era, or something like that. An interesting diversion, we enjoyed the ride twice, and the dinosaurs were just as scary the second time as they were the first. What does that tell you? Actually, they probably looked pretty big to Kumi Hiromoto. To Toshi, they resembled puppies.

After exiting through an arcade — and being informed by Eric Hiromoto that the majority of the video games were manufactured in part by their company, about which Jerry acted overly impressed — we made our way to the Bijou Theater for a live music show, a ten-minute re-creation of the highlights of the career of the Hamlet Folk, a pop-rock group of guys in different costumes who later were exposed as lip-synchers.

But first, before we could enjoy their hits, we had to stop and watch yet another reenactment of the end of a gangland criminal — in this case, Bonnie and Clyde. Hiromoto the Elder was delighted and intrigued, although his bodyguard was somewhat nervous with the gunfire and twice his hand jerked up and inside his coat, and twice I patted him on the shoulder and told him it was okay.

At the end of the play, while Bonnie and Clyde slumped over the fenders of their car (in the park's version, they get out of their vehicle and give a valiant fight — it was more exciting than just gunning them down while they were trapped inside), Hiromoto Senior leaned over to his interpreter, who then repeated the question to me.

"Why did the American G-men allow them to exit the car and shoot?"

"That's the American sense of fair play," I said. "We always let the bad guys get in the first shot, so we can say we only fired in self-defense." I smiled, but, per Harry's instructions, didn't mention Pearl Harbor.

Before Wakigama could translate Hiromoto's brow knitted in puzzlement, but he didn't respond until Waki was finished. Then his face relaxed. He nodded slowly but looked at me funny. I'm sure he wondered if I meant anything by that, but I just smiled and soon he returned it, probably figuring I was too simpleminded to be malicious.

The doors to the Bijou Theater opened and we filed in, Sally and I hanging back to let the others go first. We followed them to their choice of seating, and as we settled in, an usher tapped me on the shoulder and motioned for me to follow. I excused myself as the house lights dimmed and the curtain drew back and seven wildly dressed people trotted on stage.

I was amused to see my old buddy Bert Gibson, the former receiving gate guard, playing guitar in the backup band. I knew it was paining him terribly to be playing this music but could tell by the way he chewed his gum with his eyes closed that something else was going on. He was paying his dues, while mentally playing the blues.

While the Hiromotos and their party were being entertained in the theater under the watchful eye of two uniformed security officers, I followed the usher outside. Before I reached the exit, Sally was at my side. I gave her a questioning look, and she smiled wanly and scrunched her shoulders coyly.

"Someone will be here to meet you momentarily," the usher told us. "A Lieutenant Somebody." He went back into the Bijou.

Momentarily was an understatement. Our eyes hadn't even completely adjusted to the light when a familiar figure strode up and parked himself next to Sally.

"Good morning, Lieutenant," Sally

greeted. "My, you smell good. What is that you have on?"

Before Theo could respond, I answered for him. "It's called Eau de Lieutenant. That's French for bathroom. That's where they get the term 'loo.' Short for *loo*tenant."

"You're about as funny as a paper cut," Theo rejoined.

"So, what's new?" I asked. "Is Ozawa being good?"

"That's why I'm here. He left the house, then lost the tail in traffic. We don't know where he is, but I would guess he's headed here. This paper dropped out of his pocket as he ran to his car."

Theo handed it to me. It was a newspaper photo of Kumi Hiromoto with a slash of red ink diagonally across the businessman's face. The import of it was obvious.

"Somehow," I said, "he's going to try to kill Hiromoto."

"Where are they?"

"They're inside, watching the show. They're okay, be out in a few minutes."

"Can you contain them in one place until we find Ozawa?" Theo asked.

"I don't think they'll be happy about it, unless I tell them what's up. And park officials, meaning Harry Clark and Michelle and Jerry Opperman and the owners, would flip.

That might mess up the whole deal."

"Well, do what you can. Keep your eyes peeled. I've got some plainclothes guys coming down to help me canvas the area."

"Check the landscape shed first," I suggested.

"Too obvious. That's like looking for something where it belongs. It's the first place you look."

"So you haven't checked there yet, is that what you're saying?"

"First place we looked," he said with a grin. "I've got a guy staking it out. Oops, looks like the show's over. Back to the salt mine."

"Yeah," I agreed. "I've got it tough, don't I?"

Oh, and by the way, Sally was right. He did smell good. It wasn't his aftershave, though, it was the absence of stale smoke.

Sixteen

The Hiromoto party emerged as Theo turned to leave. I smiled and waved, and they joined me as Sally led us to our next adventure.

The rest of the crowd — if you could call it that — exited the Bijou as well, and I studied their faces, partly out of duty and partly out of curiosity. What type of people were interested in a show of this caliber? There were Americans of many nationalities, and no doubt a few foreign visitors, and most appeared glum, unimpressed, although some laughed in apparent derision. Whether it was the original Hamlet Folk and their music, this particular re-creation, or the park itself for thinking of it, something had prompted their mocking scorn. *Proletariat,* don't they know art when they see it?

A large group of smiling Asians also funneled out the double doors with the bright morning sun at their backs, chattering in their native tongue all at once, apparently delighted by the performance. They were

Koreans, I guessed, and were either visiting this country on holiday or were newly arrived immigrants. One young man with a wispy mustache and thick black glasses near the rear of the group followed in silence, carrying a leather gym bag. He looked in my direction for a second, and I thought he caught my eye, but with the sun in my eyes I couldn't be sure. At any rate, he turned away and followed his party, not paying me any heed. My imagination, I guess.

The Hiromotos were ready for more. We spent the next couple of hours having tons of fun on the rides and attractions: Solomon's Mine, the Log Ride, Shooting Gallery, watching more outdoor shoot-em-ups. Jerry Opperman was actually being civil, playing host to the guests with admirable aplomb. Maybe we finally found his niche. Guest Hostess, at minimum wage.

I kept in contact with Harry via radio, but he had nothing to report until about our tenth communiqué, as we were headed for the meeting with Everett.

"Gil, our guys found his car in the employee parking lot."

"Whose car?"

"Ozawa's."

"He's here, then," I concluded. "Any sign of him?"

"*Not yet. The police and our people are still searching.*"

"Okay. We're on our way to the rendezvous location. Be there in five."

"*Ten-four. See you — oh, wait I just remembered. Lieutenant Brown wanted me to tell you something.*"

"Go ahead."

"*That sweeper you were wondering about, he never came back to work.*"

"What do you mean?"

"*AWOL. Never called, nothing. He's been officially let go for his no-shows. Letter went out to him today.*"

"Don't expect a response," I said. "His address doesn't exist."

I signed off, then rejoined my party at an ice-cream cart and informed Kumi Hiromoto it was time to meet the real Everett, after which we could eat lunch at our world-famous, beef pot pie restaurant if he was ready. Through Waki, he told me that was fine; he was looking forward to both.

We arrived at the designated spot: a photography shop in medieval Europe where we could avail ourselves of the studio. It was set up with several dioramas — the guillotine, a peasant hovel, a castle — and after putting on the appropriate costume, guests could have their picture taken in the location of their choice. It would be ready for them when they left at the end of the day — for a whopping fee, of course.

All day long the elder Hiromoto had insisted on paying his own way, and Waki would keep track of every cent. Kumi was delighted to see that this photo would cost extra, and it dawned on me then just why he had paid for everything himself. He was projecting out his profits. What he spent, times the average number of visitors per day, times the number of days in a year, times the number of years in a — well, you get the picture.

Everett was there without a costume. Of course, Everett himself *is* a costume. But what I mean is, he wasn't wearing an outfit of any kind, just a silly twelfth-century hat, one of those colorful floppy things. A concerned Harry Clark was with him. Kumi greeted them both warmly, bowing to Everett who looked at me until I motioned for him to bow in return. He did so clumsily, in typical Everett fashion, to Hiromoto's delight.

I'd told Harry that morning not to worry, just get the best kid to play Everett, and I'd take care of the rest. I now gave Harry the "okay" sign. He didn't look relieved.

After photos were taken with Everett,

Wakigama addressed me.

"Mr. Hiromoto would now like to meet the brave young man who captured the armed robber."

"He already has," I said nonchalantly. Everyone but Sally looked at me like I'd just called Bill Clinton the greatest president this country had ever had.

"I beg your pardon, Mr. Beckman. I mean outside the costume, please."

"So do I. It was me."

"What?" said Waki.

"What?" said Harry.

"What?" said Michelle.

"Huh?" said Jerry.

I laughed. "Yes, folks, it's true. Just ask the police. They took my statement." I told them the whole story — well, most of it — and when I was done, said, "There you have it. You see, Mr. Hiromoto, it wasn't such a brave thing. A calculated risk, maybe, but not brave. I was a police officer for fifteen years. In truth, it was easy, like getting a congressman to take special interest money." I let Waki translate. "The costume allowed me to get close enough to take the gun away, and that part was the easiest. It's a simple move. I'll bet Toshi can do it, right old boy?"

Toshi looked around and nodded reluctantly, somewhat embarrassed at being the center of attention, even if only for a second.

Harry was dumbfounded and just stared. It made more sense that I would have pulled it off than some teenager. My guess was that he was a little upset that he hadn't known. "Sorry, Harry, I figured Lieutenant Brown would have told you. If not him, then Captain Fitzgerald."

"Mr. Hiromoto offers his congratulations," Wakigama said.

"Indeed," parroted Michelle dryly. She was trying hard not to be won over.

"I think I can go along with that," Eric Hiromoto said, one of his few comments of the day. "You seem to be a man of many talents, Mr. Beckman. You catch criminals, negotiate with foreign businessmen, solve mysteries, even dangle in midair upon occasion. I saw the photograph in yesterday's paper."

"There was a photo of me?" I asked rhetorically. "I didn't see it. I was out of town."

"You are a valuable man, Mr. Beckman. I trust Mr. Harry Clark appreciates your worth."

I caught Michelle's eye and winked. She didn't react.

"Oh, I certainly do," Harry lied. It was easy to tell when Harry was lying — his lips moved.

I was thinking of several smart things to say, and trying to restrain myself from saying any of them, when the Ozawa situation popped into my mind. If he was here, intending to kill Kumi Hiromoto, where would he be? He'd need to do two things: get close to Hiromoto and keep from being sighted. He'd need cover, perhaps a disguise. . . . That man with the glasses from the Bijou, perhaps?

As I considered this, my gaze came to rest on Everett, standing awkwardly in the background taking this all in. *Could it be . . . ?* I sauntered over, intending to get close enough to peek into his gaping mouth, when my radio crackled, startling me. It was the dispatcher, calling my code sign.

"Security Four here," I responded. "Go ahead."

"Lieutenant Brown wants you to report to the Dragon Control room. He has Ozawa there."

Harry heard it on his radio and nodded for me to go ahead.

"Sally and I'll be okay here," he said. "In fact, we'll all head over there in a few minutes. I believe Mr. Hiromoto wants to tame the Dragon, isn't that right?"

After Waki translated, Kumi nodded. Eric smiled but said nothing. Toshi looked none too happy.

I answered the dispatcher and took off in a trot, making it to the Dragon in just under four minutes. A young, plainclothes cop stood guard outside the door and let me in when I identified myself.

George Ozawa sat contritely in a chair, flanked by Theo and two more cops, apparently patrolmen working this detail as overtime. The narcs would have handled the surveillance but not this detail, and Theo didn't have that many young detectives.

"Did you mirandize him?" I asked Theo.

"What's the point? He's already requested an attorney, remember? We can't talk to him."

"I can." I turned to Ozawa. "So, what are you doing here, George?"

His head down, he said nothing.

"Look, Mr. Ozawa, it's clear your presence today has something to do with Kumi Hiromoto." He flinched, then stiffened, but otherwise did not respond.

"We found the photo," I went on. "It fell out of your pocket when you left your house."

Theo handed it to me, and I showed the landscaper.

"That was in my house when I returned home from the police station," he said quietly.

"Perhaps that's true, but it was you who left it there," Theo accused.

"I do not want to harm Mr. Hiromoto," Ozawa said simply and with respect.

It was time to play hardball.

"Theo, send these guys out, please." I indicated the other cops, and Theo obliged, leaving me, him, and Ozawa in the room.

"Mr. Ozawa," I continued, "in your landscaping, where only you go, we found the device that set off the charge. There is an access hole into the fireworks shack from your workroom. You have a degree in electrical engineering. Your barbecue ignitor, like the one used in the bomb, is missing. And now, with Kumi Hiromoto in the park, here you are again."

"I cannot explain any of that," he said. "I believe it is true that someone wishes Mr. Hiromoto harm. But it is not me. I have no reason."

"Oh, you have a motive, all right," I asserted. I leaned toward him. "He raped your mother in Manzanar. He is your father."

Ozawa's eye flashed, and he jumped up. "Yes, he is my father. But he did not rape my mother. He loved her. She just did not love him and was shamed by their act. She told me so on her deathbed. I wanted only to meet him, to talk to the man who is my father. I make no claim on his empire, his possessions."

"What about that photo?" Theo asked. "How do you explain that?"

"I found that newspaper photo of him when I returned home from jail. It was displayed on my kitchen table. I understood its meaning, and I came here today to warn him. And it did not fall from my pocket. I dropped it, so you would follow me here."

"Why didn't you just come to us for help?"

"Would you have believed me?"

"He's got you there," I told Theo.

"I wanted you to come, but I wanted to be by myself," Ozawa said.

"But why would someone leave that photo at your house?" Theo asked. "And why would they want you here?"

The answer came to me in a rush, and I'm sure Theo received the insight at the same time because even as he asked his question he looked up at me, startled. I put words to it.

"To take the blame. He was set up."

I thought back to the kid, the sweeper, who found the radio controller. Of course, how could I be so stupid? And as his face burned in my brain other memories returned. The man with the tattooed arms in Eric Hiromoto's offices, the long-sleeved shirt on the sweeper on a hot day, the tall man with the strange mustache — the fake mustache, I now realized — who followed the Koreans out of the Bijou . . . they were all one in the same man. Without comment, I tore out of the Dragon control room in time to see Harry, Sally, and the Hiromoto party climbing into the carts to ride the Dragon. No, Eric wasn't with them. He stood on the platform, waving. Was that a smirk on his face?

"No!" I shouted, and raced up to the control booth. "Shut it off! Now!" I waved to Sally and Harry. "Get out!"

Sally immediately responded, and dragged Harry with her. Toshi, a wiser man than he looked, literally picked his boss up and plunked him down on the loading dock, then climbed out. Waki was last and the other passengers dumbly followed, not understanding. Complaints began to build and the ride operators shrugged and apologized.

In the meantime, I began a frantic search. There had been no time to explain. Theo emerged with Ozawa, and I pointed to Eric, indicating by grabbing my own wrist that Theo was to hold him.

Then I saw my quarry. Yoshiyo Sakamura, or whatever his name was, wearing his sweeper clothes as a disguise of sorts to gain complete access to the park. That's what had been in the duffle bag. He would not be stopped by security or have his dustbin searched as he followed us around. Sakamura now stood at the edge of the pathway while people filed by. He was reaching into his dustbin, and I noticed for the first time his left pinkie was missing the last joint. *Of course,* the tattoos, the finger . . . *Yakuza.* Japanese mafia. And he worked for Eric Hiromoto.

I couldn't wait around to find out what was in the dustbin. I flew across the loading dock and dove, hitting him hard as we both went down onto the painted asphalt. Even as I was in the air, a terrifying thought flashed through my brain: *What if I was wrong?* But his dustbin clattered and opened and a radio controller slid out while my brain breathed an internal sigh of relief. Sakamura crawled for it, and I realized the Hiromotos — and Sally — were still on the loading dock and close enough to be hurt by what this time would no doubt be a full charge, large enough to blow the carts to smithereens — or beyond.

I grabbed his ankle, pain in my shoulder from my awkward landing stabbing into me, and he kicked at my face with his other foot. I saw it coming and twisted away. The blow glanced off, catching me painfully on the ear.

But as he resumed his efforts to get the controller, someone ran up and snatched it from his fingertips. It was Ozawa, who quickly inverted it and opened the battery door, letting them fall onto the ground.

Sakamura was not to be thwarted. He yanked his foot away from me and jumped up, heading for the loading dock. I was after him, but not as quickly, stinging pain and warm blood flowing from my ear. The only thing I could think of was that Sakamura had a mission to carry out, one way or the other. Even if it had to be up close and personal.

Having seen our battle, the crowd parted as Sakamura raced up the steps while a transfixed Kumi Hiromoto was left vulnerable, not understanding what was happening. That's when Toshi went to work. He moved in front of his boss, reaching into his coat, but I shouted, knowing there were too many people. At the sight of Toshi, Sakamura hesitated, and that was all I needed. I wasn't going to lose a second time. I drove my good shoulder into his lower back, knocking him into the control panel. I hit him a second time and rebounded, falling backward and to my left. I was on my way off the elevated dock, but the string of carts was there. At the last second I pushed with my legs, giving me just enough *oomph* to land on my side in a cart rather than fall all the way to the concrete underneath.

Toshi grabbed Sakamura by the neck and jerked him up, but as he did Sakamura reached out and slapped a large red button, and the string of carts shivered into motion as the shoulder harnesses automatically locked down into position . . . and I wasn't under mine.

"Jump!" Sally shouted. But I couldn't. I was on my back, my legs dangling over the side, as the string was thrown out of the dock and captured by the chain for the slow ride up the first incline.

That gave me about thirty seconds to decide what to do . . . and to do it.

Seventeen

Once I crested the top, it would be a free fall: down, up, around, over, under, bank right, bank left, upside down and turned over. And since the harness wasn't locked down in place over my shoulders, there was no way I could keep from falling out of the cart. The centrifugal force generated by the motion of the cart, although thrilling, wasn't enough to glue me to the seat without assistance, and in the loops, gravity would win out.

Halfway up the incline, I had righted myself in the seat. I tried to jam myself under the shoulder harness, but, because of the way it was constructed, I couldn't. It was built to prevent people from slipping out, so if you couldn't get out, it stood to reason you wouldn't be able to get in. And the emergency release button was out of my reach. The designers obviously hadn't foreseen this situation.

I didn't even consider just trying to hold on. Once I found out that didn't work, it would be too late to try something else. This was a one-shot deal. Being whipped from side-to-side would rip my fingers loose. And hanging upside-down? Not even a possibility.

All this flashed through my mind in a split second, and I knew my only chance of survival was to get off the ride altogether. Easier said than done. Get off how? And go where? But I couldn't even think about it. It was decision time.

I think when Paul wrote that we are to pray without ceasing, he must have envisioned a situation like this. Well, maybe not a roller coaster. Standing in the arena when the door opens and the hungry lion comes bounding out might have crossed his mind. But he wanted us to always be in an attitude of prayer, to have constant God-consciousness, so the idea of summoning up a prayer wouldn't be something we necessarily had to think about. It should be ever ready in our minds and hearts, and on our lips. And so it was with me as the carts rumbled up to the apex of the Dragon.

The first cart crested the hill. Five seconds. I crouched on the seat, one hand on the side of the cart, the other gripping the solid shoulder harness, scanning for something to grab when I jumped. I was nearly upright. Three seconds. There! About six feet below the track to the side, right at the apex, a steel mesh platform with a double guard rail, used for repairs to the gears or chain or something. I timed my jump from the moving cart. If I jumped too soon or waited too long, I'd be doing a swan dive into Ozawa's *koi* pond.

Now! With a prayer on my lips, fear in my throat, and pain in my ear and shoulder, I planted my foot and tensed my bent legs, then flexed them with all my strength and was airborne as the carts rattled over the crest and roared down the first decline. There was a scream as I jumped. Only later did I find out it was me.

An eternity passed — all two seconds of it — and I slammed into the guard rail with my abdomen. Momentum threatened to send me head first over the steel pipe but I squeezed the guard rail with my stomach muscles and jerked my knees up toward my stomach, pinning the guard rail in the middle of my curled-up body as I grasped it as best I could with my hands. I nearly spun completely around but held myself, then relaxed one hand, relocking my grip with the bar in the crook of my elbow.

For a second, I was upside down, my head and upper body outside the inadequate confines of the platform, and I fought nausea as the swirling ground seemed to rush up to meet me. Then the sky spun around, and I battled to maintain my grip and locate the floor of the platform so I could collapse onto it.

I felt it with my toe, then with both feet, as I struggled to clear my head and get rid of the dizziness. I envisioned an old silent comedy where the hero goes through all this, then, while wiping his brow at the end of his ordeal, accidentally steps off the wrong way into oblivion.

I don't know how I did it. I know I didn't see or hear angels, but that doesn't rule them out. I must have pressed my feet against the floor with my knees locked and pushed against the guard rail with my hips. At any rate, I found myself on the floor of the platform in a heap, gripping the edge until my fingers hurt and looking through the steel mesh, just knowing I could ooze through the tiny holes and reassemble on the bottom side to plummet once again.

Now that had been an "E" ticket ride!

How long I stayed there, worshiping the Lord with all prayer and supplication, I don't know. While not letting go, I finally opened my eyes to reorient myself.

It would take a minute to regain my legs, then I'd have to find a way down. As I took silent stock in my physical condition, I heard my name and someone calling up, asking if I was okay. I tried to answer but realized my throat was dry, and the words wouldn't come. I waved weakly, but the message was received. I ached all over from the tensing of my body to hold on. I also shook from the adrenaline.

Venturing a look down, I saw everyone on the loading dock and hundreds of other guests all watching me. I had become an attraction. I waved again, more vigorously, and received a spontaneous ovation from the appreciative masses.

Toshi held Sakamura by the neck, even though he'd already been handcuffed. Ozawa was off to the side, looking at Kumi Hiromoto with an expression I couldn't make out from this distance, but he didn't take his eyes off the elderly Japanese businessman.

Sally was next to Theo, who had his arm around her for support. It was then I noticed Jerry Opperman by himself at the far end of the loading dock, staring at the handcuffed Eric Hiromoto, who ignored him while glaring with an air of haughty detachment at . . . his grandfather? George Ozawa? The cops? I was too far away to be sure.

Enough of that. I had to get down. I leaned over the edge of the platform and saw that the pillar to which it was attached, and which supported the track, had steel spikes jutting out on either side every couple feet alternately, like those on a telephone pole. I couldn't wait for the fire department; I'd had enough of heights for awhile.

I almost laughed out loud when I realized I'd been on this roller coaster twice and still hadn't made it all the way around.

Taking a deep breath, then another, I pressed myself up, steadying myself with a hard grip on the top rail, wiped my palms one at a time on my thighs, and climbed over to begin my descent.

I descended slowly, keeping my eyes and concentration fixed on the spikes. I remembered when I used to work graveyard patrol for the P.D. and had to climb onto the roofs of single-story businesses when their alarms went off to make sure they hadn't been broken into through a roof hatch. Going up was easy. It was climbing down those fifteen-foot ladders that gave me the willies. If only they could see me now.

I shook all over, unable to quell it, and hoped it wasn't enough to make me slip. That's all it would take — one slip. Because Joey had climbed the structure at another location, he hadn't had the benefit of the climbing aids, and I appreciated his accomplishment all the more.

By the time I reached the ground, I could hardly swallow. Two uniformed security officers were there to meet me, offering assistance. I actually felt like being carried but in a brave show of self-sufficiency, waved them off with a *no thank you.* I asked for something to drink, though, and by the time I reached the loading dock, someone had pressed a plastic Everett into my hands. I drained the sweet cherry-flavored liquid in a single breath, the suction as I repeatedly swallowed making Everett's belly move in and out.

Then I strode over to Sakamura to punch him out.

Theo sensed my anger — I believe the steam whistling out of my ears and my clenched fists gave me away — and quickly told his partners to haul the suspect to the slammer.

"You're a Christian," he whispered to me, throwing a wet blanket over my righteous indignation.

Sally came over and took me in her arms again.

"This is getting old," I said.

"Me hugging you?" she asked.

"No, what I have to go through to get you to hug me. Hanging in space, closer to my Maker than I care to be at this early stage of my life. If it happens one more time, I'm going to England with Trish."

"Over my dead body," Sally said, with no equivocation whatsoever in her tone.

I smiled.

"Look here, Lieutenant!" a park security officer shouted. He was under the string of carts I had been on, which were now resting at the dock with the power off.

Theo hopped down to look at what I presumed to be a bomb — a big one this time — and I started to go too, but Sally held on.

"Enough, Gil. Let him take care of it."

I sighed. She was right. It was time to step aside finally and let the cops do their work.

Spectators the whole while, Kumi Hiromoto and his translator, Mr. Wakigama, approached me to offer their congratulations, or so I figured. They stood by humbly, waiting for Sally and me to unwind.

I let go, and Sally instinctively began to back away, but I caught her hand and kept her next to me. I acknowledged the elder Hiromoto.

"Hiromoto-*san* says he is in your debt and greatly appreciates your bravery," Wakigama said, lapsing suddenly into more formal speech.

"Thank you, sir," I said, looking directly at Hiromoto. Kumi said something to Waki, who repeated it to me.

"He does not understand what has happened today and why his grandson went with the police. Perhaps Beckman-*san* can enlighten us as to the nature of these events and why his grandson is being treated as a common criminal like the other man."

Jerry Opperman suddenly pushed his way in and voiced his own objections.

"I'm outraged at your conduct, Buckman! Consider yourself fi—"

Toshi grabbed him by the collar and dragged him back, then spoke to him in hushed tones that sent Opperman off the platform and out of sight, his forked tail tucked between his legs. From her position a short distance away, Michelle smiled and continued to watch the drama unfold.

"I'll do my best," I said. I leaned over and whispered to Sally, and she slipped away. I returned my attention to Hiromoto. "The young man I was fighting works for your grandson — no, that's okay, Mr. Wakigama, you don't have to translate. Your boss speaks English. He understands me." I locked eyes with Hiromoto, almost challenging him.

He returned my stare, then slowly broke into an embarrassed smile.

"How did you know, Mr. Beckman?"

"You reacted before Mr. Wakigama translated a few times. Besides, a man like yourself, with so many . . . interests, shall we say, in the United States, would do well to speak English. Mainly, though, I knew you spoke English because you lived here in your youth. In fact, you were interned for a time in Manzanar and Tule Lake, were you not?"

"Yes, that is true, but I don't see —"

"Something happened there, Mr. Hiromoto, that continues to have repurcussions. That young fellow who wanted to kill you works for your grandson. He is *yakuza*. You must know your grandson is involved."

He hung his head. "Yes, I suspected so. But he has been in America many years, and I did not keep track of him as I should. So this was an attempt to remove me and take over control of Hiro Industries. But why? I am old. It would be Eric's soon anyway."

"Eric didn't think so," I said. "There was someone in his way."

"There is no one. His father is dead."

"Yes, but not his uncle."

"I have no other son."

Sally returned, holding a subdued George Ozawa by the arm.

"Kumi Hiromoto," I said, "may I present your son, George Ozawa, born to Sachiko Takada in Manzanar."

The men looked at each other, both stunned at finally meeting face to face. It was a day they had longed for, each in his own way and for his own reasons, yet neither one would display the overt emotion these kind of reunions usually engender. Kumi's eyes filled, but he remained stoic.

I whispered to Toshi, and he guided Hiromoto while I led George Ozawa, taking them both into the Dragon breakroom which had emptied during the fight. We closed the door behind us as we backed out, shook hands, and I left Toshi standing guard.

After a brief conversation with Theo and Michelle, Sally and I were taken via electric cart to First Aid to get my ear looked at. I'd go for X rays on my shoulder later, but I didn't think anything was broken.

"I don't get it," Sally said while the nurse treated my ear. "Why would Eric do this?"

"He wanted Ozawa out of the way, afraid that Ozawa would come forth to claim an inheritance. So he set out to kill two birds with one stone — get rid of Grandpa and let Ozawa take the blame. It was probably Eric who bailed Ozawa out and planted that photo in his home to draw him to the park. Of course, Sakamura probably did the actual dirty work. What bothers me is, we almost played into it."

"Almost only counts in horseshoes and

hand grenades, you always tell me," Sally pointed out.

"This was a little like a hand grenade," I said, "only bigger."

"How did Eric find out about George?"

"I don't know, but I'd wager it was when his own father died in the plane crash. There must have been some papers or letters or something. Eric could have traced Ozawa to the park easily — after all, he wasn't trying to hide — and that might have spawned the whole idea of the Nagasaki expansion. Michelle just told me it was Eric who first approached Opperman with the idea."

"Then building a park in Japan wasn't really going to happen?"

"Maybe not at first. But Kumi was taken with the idea — even though he didn't know Ozawa worked here — and he especially liked Everett."

"I still don't understand. Why the trial bomb before Mr. Hiromoto got here?"

"To set the bloodhounds on a false trail. The fact is, the radio controller was probably never in the bushes. Sakamura just said it was. Or he left it there and the police missed it, which would explain why he had to 'find' it and give it to us. He's clever, though. He didn't give it directly to us, which would have been too obvious. He gave it to Dave Whelan to turn in, so we could 'discover' it."

"What if you hadn't?"

I smiled wryly. "No chance," I said. "Seriously, I'm sure he would have thought of something else. Perhaps we already had missed it. Maybe it was in the bushes all the time, and the police just didn't find it, so he had to give it to us. But it worked, so I guess we'll never know what plan C was."

The rear door to First Aid opened, and Theo sauntered in.

"How's the ear, Van Gogh?" he asked.

"No problem," I said. "*I* can grow my hair long to cover it."

Theo absentmindedly ran a hand over his own thinning locks. "You know, we're not going to be able to charge Eric. We've got no proof he had anything to do with it."

"Sakamura isn't talking?"

"Are you kidding? These are people who cut off their fingers to atone for dishonoring each other. They don't talk."

"But Eric knew his grandfather would ride the Dragon. He told me so."

"Still not enough to prosecute, and you know it."

"Now what?"

"Well, I called the State Department. They're trying to see if there's enough to revoke his visa. But I think Mr. Hiromoto

316

— senior, that is — will take care of it. When I explained it all to him, he looked mighty upset. He doesn't go for this *yakuza* business."

"He was a Black Dragon."

"Yeah, but that was different. Based on what you told me, that was for freedom from American imperialism and a protest against the war relocation centers. The *yakuza* is just a greed thing. Crime spawned by greed."

"How's Michelle?"

"She's fine — now that she understands everything. She said to tell you thanks."

I nodded, wondering if that would help me get a decent assignment. Probably not.

"Well, that's about it, then," I said. "I don't know about you, but I'm ready for a vacation."

"Yeah, I can imagine," Theo agreed. "Why don't you go spend a week in Florida . . . at Disneyworld?"

"Funny."

"Seriously, Gil. Before you take off for parts unknown, could we talk? I've been thinking about what you told me the other day, and I have some questions."

"Sure, Theo. Why don't you come over tomorrow afternoon?"

"Okay. See you then. I think I've got enough on this one to write the report without your help. Go get yourself taken care of. And you, Sally, maybe you ought to consider staying closer to him. Keep him out of trouble."

"Yes sir," she said with a smile, and after Theo waved and left, she squeezed my arm. "I think you're getting through to him," she said.

"No, Sally, God's getting through to him."

We stood in a circle around Trish at a departure gate in the international terminal of the airport . . . Sally and me and Harold and Estelle Curran. Trish's flight had just been called, and we exchanged our last hugs and shed some more tears — not me and Harold, of course, just the emotional women. Well, okay, my eyes watered a little.

Trish was just about to retreat down the loading ramp when she suddenly stopped and reached into her bag.

"I almost forgot," she said. She laughed a little, wiped a tear off her cheek with the back of her hand, then pulled out an envelope, which she handed to me. "Daddy said to give you this."

"What is it?" I asked. I took it and lifted the flap, and peeked inside, then looked back up at Trish, stunned. "I don't get it."

"Oh, yes you do. That's exactly the point. You do get it."

"W-why?"

"It's no good to me. I can't take it with me. Daddy says it's a little thank you from him. And me."

"I can't take it," I stammered.

"Sure you can, Gil. It's not much, being used and all."

"But —"

"Please, no arguments." She stepped over to me and kissed me on the cheek, then turned to Sally. "Make sure he takes care of it."

"I will," she assured. "I will."

Trish spun around and retreated down the ramp leading to the plane without further comment, leaving me holding the keys and the pink slip to the BMW.

"Did you know about this?" I asked Sally. She only smiled.

And yes, I did cry this time. Who wouldn't?

As we walked through the airport, I said quietly to Sally, "Did she leave me the cellular phone, too? Ow! I was just kidding."

Author's Note

If you are ever driving on U.S. Highway 395 through California's magnificent Owens Valley, in the shadow of Mount Whitney, take some time to stop in the town of Independence. Turn west from the courthouse, which is on the main highway through town, and you'll drive right into the parking lot of the Eastern California Museum. Browse through the Manzanar section, inspect the photos, and examine the artifacts. You'll be amazed and surprised at how different Manzanar and the other camps were from what we generally believe, but more so by the undying spirit of the people who called Manzanar home . . . people who not only went through a valley of weeping but made it into a spring.